"Just relax."

Brant shot her a grin. "This isn't an audition. We're two friends having a jam session."

She nodded and turned back to the piano and began to play.

Brant began singing. He knew the words by heart, but he stood behind Tori as if he needed the hymnal. He wanted to be close to her. She'd obviously had it rough and he found himself wanting to soothe her pain.

As she played the second verse, she visibly relaxed. When she finished, she turned to face him again. Brant applauded.

"You're great, Tori!"

"I haven't played like that in years."

"So what do you say. Will you play at church?"

She blinked. "I guess. If the congregation is willing to have me."

"I'm certain they'll be as enamored with you as I am."

She blushed and his face heated.

"I mean—enamored with

But that wasn't all he

D0802712

Books by Shannon Taylor Vannatter

Love Inspired Heartsong Presents

Rodeo Regrets
Rodeo Queen
Rodeo Song
Rodeo Family

SHANNON TAYLOR VANNATTER

is a stay-at-home mom/pastor's wife/award-winning author. She lives in a rural central Arkansas community with a population of around 100, if you count a few cows. Contact her at shannonvannatter.com.

SHANNON TAYLOR VANNATTER

Rodeo Family

HEARTSONG
PRESENTS

Recycling programs
for this product may
not exist in your area.

™ LOVE INSPIRED BOOKS

ISBN-13: 978-0-373-48765-3

Rodeo Family

Copyright © 2015 by Shannon Taylor Vannatter

www.Harlequin.com

Printed in U.S.A.

But God commendeth his love toward us, in that, while we were yet sinners, Christ died for us.
—*Romans* 5:8

To ACFW Arkansas members Nichole Hall,
Lisa Collins, Kimberly Buckner, Jenny Carlisle,
Rosie Baldwin, Ann McCauley, Hannah Wood
and Debbie Sheetrum for jiggling my brain loose
when I got stuck on this series. I hope to see
each of your names on book covers soon.

Acknowledgments

I appreciate DeeDee Barker-Wix, Director of Sales
at the Cowtown Coliseum, former Aubrey City Hall
secretary Nancy Trammel-Downes, Aubrey
Main Street Committee member Deborah Goin,
Aubrey librarian Kathy Ramsey,
and Steve and Krys Murray, owners of
Moms on Main for all their help and support.

Deep gratitude for their legal help goes to
attorney Raymond Boyles and Wesley Harris,
a 37-year police veteran and writer's consultant
on police matters. Any mistakes are mine.

Chapter 1

Weights pressed down on Tori's eyelids. Her head ached. She examined her tender lips with her tongue. Swollen. Split. A moan escaped her.

What happened?

She strained to open her eyes until one lid lifted. The other wouldn't budge. All she saw was a sideways view of the living room from her reclining position on the couch.

Oh yeah. Now she remembered.

She wiggled her fingers and toes to make sure she still could, then raised her hand to her face. Gingerly, she touched her eye and gasped. A massive, throbbing bulge.

How had she ended up like this—just like her mother—beaten and bruised?

Someone pounded at the door. She sat upright. Had he left? If so, was he back? Was he still mad? Her gaze darted to the back door. Could she escape? Or would he only catch up with her and punish her more?

Besides, where would she go? She hadn't bothered to get to know her neighbors in tiny Aubrey, Texas. The only person she knew was her boss. And her boss was at work where Tori was supposed to be. She covered her face with her hands.

"Tori, I know you're in there," Jenna Steele, her boss, called. "Your car's in the drive and I can see your purse through the window."

Okay, so her boss wasn't at work. What time was it?

Still daylight, but dimming. It had to be after the store closed. Jenna must be on her way home.

She held her breath. Russ must have left. Or passed out.

Please go away. Jenna—the paragon of virtue—couldn't see her like this. And what if Russ woke up or came back? She couldn't let him hurt Jenna—the only person who hadn't given up on her.

Other than Aunt Loretta.

"Just a minute." Head pounding, she got to her feet. A wave of nausea hit her followed by swimming vision in her good eye. Clutching a bookshelf, she waited until it passed and shuffled toward the door.

"I'm fine, Jenna, just sick. I don't want you to catch it. I'm sorry I didn't call in this morning."

"I'm not leaving until you open the door. We need to talk and if you're that sick, you might need to see your doctor. It is flu season."

Even though Jenna was probably miffed with her for missing so much work lately, concern tinged her voice. If Tori didn't answer, Jenna was likely to call the Texas Rangers, especially since her cousin was married to one.

But if Tori answered, Jenna might still call the Texas Rangers. Either way, she was toast.

"You have to promise me you won't call the police."

Silence for a moment. "Why would I call the police? Tori, you're scaring me."

"You have to promise. It will only make things worse if the police get involved."

"I don't see how that can be, but I promise."

Tori unlocked the door and swung it open.

Horror flashed in Jenna's contorted expression. Her hand flew to her mouth. "Who did this to you?"

Tori shook her head. Pain knifed through her head and she swayed.

"Sit down." Jenna took her arm, led her to the couch and headed to the kitchen.

Cabinet doors and drawers squeaked open and slammed shut. Ice clinked in a glass. Jenna was back a few minutes later.

Something cold touched Tori's swollen eye and she winced.

"Sorry. Should have warned you."

Her good eye singed and a tear slipped past her lashes.

"Is it possible whoever did this will come back?"

A sob escaped as Tori nodded.

"Then, let's get out of here."

"Where?" Tori bit the inside of her lip until she tasted blood. "I don't want Aunt Loretta involved in this. I don't have anywhere else to go."

"I do." Jenna helped Tori up.

"I can't go with you. He'll come after me. I've tried to break it off with him before." This morning to be exact. Maybe the day after Valentine's hadn't been the best plan. But she'd thought if she broke it off this morning when she was expected at work, he wouldn't hit her. Wrong.

"I live on a private ranch with five houses, an electronic gate with a top secret password and an alarm system. If *he* comes after you, we'll know it before he figures out which house you're in. And we have our very own Texas Ranger less than a mile away."

Tori blew out a breath. "I don't want to involve you."

"I'm already involved." Jenna moved the ice pack. "Go grab some clothes. We'll come back later and get the rest."

Obviously, Jenna wasn't going anywhere without her. If they didn't get moving, Russ would come back. And hurt Jenna too.

Brant McConnell punched in the code his friend, Garrett Steele had given him and rubbed a hand across bleary eyes. Past midnight. He'd be glad in the morning with the short drive to church.

The iron gate slid open and Brant drove through—for seemingly endless miles before he saw a road that turned to the right. He took the road and drove more endless miles. Trees lined the fence along each side of the drive and the dark shapes of horses dotted the miles of pasture-land. Some spread, Garrett.

Nine years ago, they'd both tried to catch a break in the Christian music industry in Nashville. Brant had given up after a year and come back home, while Garrett hit it big in Country music. But Garrett's life had spun out of control.

If he'd stayed in the music industry, would Brant have strayed from God, too? He'd bided his time as the song leader at his church. Until Garrett called a few months ago.

With his life straightened out, Garrett had headlined at Cowtown Coliseum opening the Fort Worth Stockyards Championship Rodeo for two months. And paved the way for Brant to follow in his footsteps. As if everything were falling into place with divine purpose, Garrett's church also needed a song director. Surely his big break at a mega-church would be just around the arena.

Finally, Brant caught a glimpse of a darkened house with a green metal roof. He pulled in the drive, parked and opened his door. An owl hooted a greeting, then quieted as a pack of coyotes yapped in the distance. Oh, the sounds of the country—always made him feel right at home. He slung his guitar over his shoulder, grabbed his overnight bag and elbowed the door shut.

The rustic porch with pine posts and a swing invited him to sit a spell. As the chorus of coyotes moved out of earshot he imagined having coffee there in the morning.

Silence measured in seconds. The brave owl tentatively hooted as Brant made his way to the door. The key Garrett had given him at church clicked in the lock. He pushed the door open and flipped on the light.

White stucco walls, an Austin stone fireplace, with log beams lining the ceiling. Rustic hardwood floors and leather furnishings. Nice crib. And this was only the guesthouse. Brant set his gear down and headed down the hall.

A darkened room to his right. The bedroom? He stopped in the doorway and ran his hand over the wall to find the switch. A floorboard creaked. He stiffened. Someone lurked in the shadows.

"Don't move," a female voice ordered.

"I'm not here to hurt anyone." His finger grazed the light switch and he flipped it on.

"I mean it." Some of the confidence in her tone wavered as light flooded the room. "I'll brain you right out of Texas."

A small strawberry blonde wielded a fire poker poised to strike. And she was sporting one humdinger of a black eye.

Lord, help.

She didn't say anything, but started to cry.

He slipped his hands up in surrender. "I'm Brant McConnell, a friend of Garrett's. We were roommates in Nashville."

"What are you doing here?" Despite her weapon, her voice cracked.

"Garrett said I could crash here so I wouldn't have to drive so far to church in the morning."

"From Nashville." Sarcasm dripped from her words.

"I live in Fort Worth now." He backed away from her. "I won't hurt you. I promise. I'll just go back to my truck, and call Garrett. There must have been some mix-up. Obviously, I'm at the wrong house."

He backed out of the room, scooped up his guitar and overnight bag, and headed for the door. From the looks of her, she might come after him.

Who'd given her the shiner? It certainly hadn't been a cabinet door. Could have been a bar fight with another woman. But it looked like more than the average woman's strength could inflict. And she was too tiny to be the brawler type. Probably some jerk Brant would like to get his hands on. His gut twisted. He didn't cotton to a man laying a finger on a woman. Much less a fist.

What now? He didn't even know where Garrett's house was on the property and it was too late to show up on his doorstep anyway.

Drive back to Fort Worth? Should have stayed there. The encounter had jarred him awake, but how long would the adrenalin last? He needed to at least get away from the house so the battered redhead could relax. He started the truck, backed out of the drive and turned toward the gate, hating to think of her alone—crying.

A mile or so down the road, he pulled to the side. Wouldn't be the first time he slept in his truck.

He slumped down and tried to get comfortable. Could sleep in the pickup bed, but it'd get awful hard and chilly before morning.

Lights illuminated his cab from behind. He turned around as another truck approached.

Please not the redhead coming to clobber him with her poker.

The truck stopped beside him. He rolled his window down as a man got out.

"Brant?" Garrett called.

"Hey." Brant covered a yawn. "I didn't mean to wake up the whole neighborhood. I was gonna sleep here."

"No way. Sorry about the houseguest. She just arrived today and I didn't even think about you coming in tonight since you've never taken me up on my offer before."

"I should have called, but I didn't decide until after the rodeo. By then it was late."

"Turn around here and you can follow me to the house."

"I don't want to disturb Jenna. I'll get a hotel in Denton."

"Nonsense, you're staying with us. Besides, Jenna's with Tori, the houseguest. She called to see if you were for real and since she was upset, Jenna went over." Garrett got back in his truck.

Brant backed his pickup around and followed Garrett back down the tree-lined drive. What was the houseguest's story?

She was a beauty—even with the shiner. What could possess a man to hit a defenseless woman? His chest boiled.

Garrett stayed straight instead of turning right toward the guesthouse and Brant followed. What seemed like countless miles later, Garrett's brake lights came on. Their headlights illuminated the sprawling Spanish style stucco house with a red clay roof. Some house.

Brant parked, got out and unloaded his guitar and overnight bag again. "Sorry I scared your houseguest. She was crying when I left. Waving a fire poker at me, but crying."

"Jenna will probably stay with her."

"What's her story?"

"She's an interior designer—works at the Fort Worth store for Jenna." Garrett shrugged. "I don't really know her story—other than she's not a Christian and if not for her, Jenna and I might not be together."

"How's that?"

"Tori dragged Jenna to my concert that started it all." Garrett headed for the house and Brant followed.

"Any idea who hit her?"

"She hasn't told us yet. She's called in sick a lot lately, including today, so Jenna stopped by her place after work. Seems she's in an abusive relationship. Jenna managed to get her to stay here at least for the night and she promised to go to church with us once her face heals up. So be praying for her."

"I will." He already had. The moment he'd seen her eye.

Wednesday. Five days since the beating and with a ton of makeup to cover the bruising, Tori had made it to work for two days in a row now. She moved a bronze Texas longhorn statue to the center of the window display to catch the light better.

She'd let Jenna down so much lately, but that was over. Russ was out of her life, didn't even know where she was. The only problem, she'd have to go back to her rental house eventually. She couldn't stay in Jenna's guesthouse indefinitely. And when she did go home, would he show up?

Tori shivered. A distant memory flashed through her mind—her mom slamming into the wall. Her dad going after her again, stopping as he saw Tori peeping through her cracked-open bedroom door.

"What are you looking at, you little tramp?" he barked.

She shut the door and slid to the floor, her hands clamped over her ears. Until the noise stopped. He'd left or passed out—she couldn't remember which—and she'd tended her mom's wounds like she always did.

That was the last beating. The next day when she came home from school, she'd found her mom in the tub with her wrists slashed. Wounds she couldn't tend. Tori was just fifteen.

"I'll be in the office." Jenna touched her arm, jerking her back to the present. "Let me know if it gets busy again."

"Sure." Tori forced a smile.

"You okay?"

"Fine."

"You can't even see it anymore. Does it still hurt?"

"It's just bruised now."

"We'll get you through this." Jenna squeezed her elbow and turned toward the storeroom.

Tori's vision blurred. Jenna had been so good to her. And gotten nothing in return but grief.

How had she ended up with Russ? A man so much like her father.

For the first time all day, the store had slowed. She picked up the feather duster and swished it over dozens of lamps, sculptures and works of art.

The bell dinged and she turned.

A massive man wearing a ball cap filled the doorway.

Russ.

Chapter 2

Tori's mouth went dry. She froze in place. Why had she never thought of him coming here? Because in the three weeks since he'd moved in, he'd never once come to see her at work. He'd only cared about her bed and using her as a punching bag.

But no more. Done. She was done. Just like that Country song she liked.

Just keep him calm. And deal with him later.

"Cat got your tongue?" he sneered, his words slurring together.

Drunk. Which made him even more volatile.

"What can I do for you, Russ?"

"For starters, you can come home. Where you been, babe?"

The endearment made her skin crawl. How had she put up with him as long as she had? Simple. He terrified her.

"I really can't talk now. I'm working."

He scanned the store. "Nope. Don't see any customers."

"But my boss is in the back. We'll have to discuss this later."

"We'll discuss it now." He took a menacing step toward her.

"Really, Russ, you need to go." She hated the quiver in her voice. "You'll get me fired."

"And you're bluffing. Nobody's here but us." He ran a finger over a lampshade, then whacked his hand into the base creating a domino effect of falling lamps. Glass shattered and flew while rawhide shades tumbled in a heap.

"Please stop." Tori clamped her hands over her ears.

Russ picked up a large piece of glass, ran his fingers across the jagged edge and took another step toward her.

"Hold it right there." Jenna stepped out of the storeroom, holding a large bronze statue above her head with both hands. "I just called 911 and the store next door to round up as many burly cowboys as possible and send them over. So I suggest you stay put."

The door opened and six cowboys trooped in as Jenna scurried to Tori's side. Two of the men blocked the door while the others created a barrier between Russ and the two women.

"This guy bothering you ladies?"

Tori couldn't tell which cowboy had spoken, but his voice sounded familiar.

"Yes." Jenna still held her statue like a weapon. "I called 911. If you could detain him until the police arrive."

Russ bolted for the back, but one of the cowboys cut him off.

"Didn't you want to say something to him, Tori?" Jenna elbowed her.

Tori's mouth opened, but nothing came out for a second. "Done. We're over. Done."

"Got that?" The man with the familiar voice jabbed a finger at Russ. "She doesn't want to see you again. And we don't want to see you round here again. Got that?"

Mitch Warren and another officer rushed in the front door, hands on holstered guns, obviously not sure who the suspect was.

"Right here's our troublemaker, Mitch." Jenna pointed to Russ. "I want this man arrested for vandalism and terroristic threats."

"No, Jenna. Please." Tori breathed the plea. "It will only make things worse."

"If this loser is in jail, he can't take his frustrations out on innocent victims."

"What's going on, Jenna?" Mitch asked.

"This man threatened my employee and broke my lamps."

Mitch, Jenna's cousin's Texas Ranger husband, turned to Tori. "Is that true?"

"He didn't really threaten me."

"He cornered you, Tori." Jenna blew out a frustrated sigh. "With a big piece of glass from the lamps he broke. He frightened you. That's a threat in my book."

"Did anyone else see what happened?"

"They came in after the fact." Jenna set her statue down, as if she'd just realized she still held a potential weapon. "I called the store next door and asked the owner to round up some men to keep him under control until y'all got here."

"He had her cornered when we got here and he *was* holding a big piece of broken glass." The familiar leader backed up Jenna's claim. "And then he tried to bolt out the back."

"And I've got it all on tape thanks to my security camera." Jenna played her trump card with a satisfied grin.

With the men who'd come for backup sidetracked, no one covered the door. Russ bolted.

"Whoa, hold it right there." Mitch cut him off and Russ threw a punch, but his fist only met air as he wobbled.

"I didn't do nothing." Russ growled. "The tramp ain't worth the effort."

Tori clamped her hands over her ears.

Mitch cuffed Russ.

But she knew he wouldn't be locked up long. And when he got out, he'd come after her.

Just like the time she and her mom had slipped out in the

middle of the night so long ago. But her dad found them. And her mom had paid with that last beating.

And her life.

The bell above the door jingled as Mitch led Russ out. The familiar man turned to face her.

The man from the other night. The one she'd pulled the poker on.

"You hungry?" Brant's bootheels tapped across the brick-lined streets of the Fort Worth Stockyards.

"Not really." Tori strode beside him, hugging herself.

The sixty degree temp drew locals and tourists to the historic district. The locals wore cowboy or cowgirl gear. The tourists wore cameras.

"Jenna said to feed you. I don't want to have to answer to her later."

"My stomach's all in a jumble. If I ate something, I'd probably hurl."

"Understandable." He let the rest of their trek to his truck fall into silence.

He'd given his official statement then waited outside while Mitch spoke with the other witnesses. Eventually, Jenna had come outside with Tori and asked him to take her home.

Tori, still shaking, had insisted she was fine. But Jenna was more insistent.

"Here's my truck." He opened the door for her.

"I really can drive myself. No sense in you driving me all the way to Aubrey."

"You seem shaky to me and it's not that far. Besides, it's church night. I was planning to head there after I did my shopping."

She hesitated a second, then climbed in.

He was glad he kept his truck clean. No fast food sacks

or manure in the floorboard. Not in his truck. He shut her door and rounded the vehicle.

As he started the engine, he scanned her wounded eye and profile. "That jerk the one who did that to you?"

"I don't want to talk about it."

He grazed her cheek with the back of his fingers and she flinched. "I'm not gonna hurt you. I don't hurt women. I just wanna see your eye." Still a bit puffy and yellow bruising her makeup didn't quite cover. He gently cupped her chin and turned her to face him. "Looks a lot better. Did you ever see a doctor?"

"No."

"Should've. A blow like that could've cracked your eye socket. And if you'd seen a doctor, you'd have evidence for the police."

"I'm not pressing charges." She shuddered.

"Why not?"

"He'd only get out and come back madder. I wish Jenna hadn't pressed charges."

"If nobody presses charges, a jerk like that will keep shoving people around." He traced her cheekbone. "Hurting women. He needs to be stopped."

"Men like him can't be stopped." She pulled out of his grasp. "Sorry you got caught up in this."

"I'm not. I never mind rescuing damsels in distress. My white horse was getting bored."

A tiny smile curved her pretty lips. "How did you end up in my little drama?"

"I was in the gift shop next door looking for a birthday gift for my sister."

"Did you find something?"

"I'll come back another day. So, it's four o'clock and I skipped lunch. How about an early supper?"

"Can you take me home now? I mean to the guesthouse." Her laugh came out harsh. "I guess I don't have a home anymore."

His gut twisted. Hurt, hunted, homeless. Made him want to protect her. Keep her safe. "You sure you don't want anything to eat?"

"Maybe drive through McDonald's. My mom used to take me to McDonald's to cheer me up after…"

He waited for her to finish, but she didn't. After what?

"Want to stop here or in Denton?"

"Denton. That way it'll stay warm on the drive to the guesthouse."

"I don't let just anybody eat in my truck, but you can eat in my truck anytime."

Another tiny smile escaped. "Thanks, but I'll wait. Maybe by the time we get to the guesthouse, my stomach will settle."

He scanned her profile again wanting to know more about her. What had gotten her to this point? She tugged at something deep inside him. Something that wanted to make sure that jerk never got close enough to hurt her again.

Tori nibbled on her Filet-O-Fish on the front porch swing. Brant sat on the floor, leaning against an Austin stone pillar. As he wolfed down his Big Mac, his gaze barely left her.

"Are you supervising me?" Tori took a sip of her shake. "You really can go anytime. I'm fine."

"I told you, I don't want to tangle with Jenna. I'm making sure you eat. Besides, I have time to kill before church."

"So you met Garrett in Nashville?"

"Right after high school. We met at church, realized we were chasing the same dream and got an apartment together."

"You're a musician?" She winced as the unintended bitterness in her tone turned the word ugly.

"Guilty. Garrett stuck it out, but I went home after a year to Pleasant Valley, Texas—near Wichita Falls."

"What brought you to Fort Worth?" Tori dropped her empty sandwich box into the paper bag beside her.

"While Garrett was doing his two-month headliner gig at the Stockyards, he recommended me." Brant finished his meal and wadded his trash in a ball. "My sister is a school nurse in Garland. I've wanted to live closer to her since her husband died a few years ago."

"He must have been young." Tori pushed off with one foot, sending the swing into a jerky diagonal movement. Just like her life—off-kilter. She clamped her French fry container tighter between her knees. "What happened?"

"He was a Texas Ranger, Mitch Warren's partner." Brant's ironic laugh sounded more like a grunt. "But he died in an off duty car wreck."

"That's so sad." And she meant it. She knew how it felt to lose someone you love.

"It was tough on her. Especially since their son was only three. But she's trying to follow through on their plans to raise him in a small town. She applied for the school nurse position at Aubrey and we were looking to buy Jenna's house together, but she didn't get the job."

"Has she applied anywhere else? Plenty of small towns, doctor's offices and hospitals around here." Tori popped a French fry in her mouth and turned sideways on the swing, stretching her legs out on the seat.

"She wants to work at a school, so her hours match her boy's, but none of the other smaller schools have openings."

"Do you still want to be a music star?" Her voice quivered. She pushed off the porch rail behind her and set the swing in motion again.

"Not like you're thinking, but I am hoping it will lead to something bigger." He caught her gaze. "What's your story, Tori?"

Despite everything, his unintentional rhyme got a grin out of her. But where to begin on her story—as if she even wanted to. She closed her eyes. "You don't want to know."

"Really. I do. Maybe someday, you'll decide you want me to know."

He was too good to be true. She'd never told anyone her story. He probably wouldn't believe her if she did.

"Can I at least know your last name?"

"Eaton. Go ahead."

"What?"

"Give me your best joke about Tori Eaton eatin' French fries."

He grinned. "I'm no good with jokes when I'm trying. You going to church tonight?" His voice was soft, gentle.

Something stirred deep inside Tori. Jenna had dragged her to church over a year ago and something had stirred then, yet she'd walked away and vowed to never go back. But after Russ and the mess she'd gotten herself into, maybe God was the only one left to turn to.

"I promised Jenna I'd go when I got presentable enough." She gingerly touched the skin under her eye. "Swelling's gone. Still a little red and yellow."

"Nobody would notice if they didn't know what happened. And for the record, you were presentable last week. Even with your shiner and fire poker."

Something tightened in her throat. Why was he being so nice to her? The same way Jenna had always gone above and beyond to be kind to her. Could their God make her like them?

"I think I will go."

Brant's eyes lit up as if she'd handed him a million dollars. "Great! Want to ride with me?" He cleared his throat.

"I mean, we're both headed to the same place. And it's not like you have a car handy."

"Thanks, but I need to put a fresh coat of makeup on my eye." She stopped the swing and stood. "I'm sure Jenna and Garrett will give me a ride."

"I can wait. I mean, since I'm already here and all. Save them a stop."

She bit her lip. Five days ago, as she lay on the floor after Russ's beating, she'd sworn off men. But Brant was unlike any man she'd ever known. Could she really trust him?

"What should I wear?"

He scanned her black slacks and jacket paired with a black-and-white-striped top and heels. Quick. Not the way most men looked her up and down. And his interest was obviously only on her attire.

How had she not noticed his jade eyes before now? Such a contrast against his sun-bronzed skin, short dark hair, and close-clipped beard.

"I'm wearing what I've got on. We're casual on Wednesday night."

"Let me freshen up." She picked up her bag of trash, retrieved his and headed for the door. "Want to wait inside?"

"I'm fine here. Take your time. I've still got a good forty-five minutes before I need to be there and it's just down the road from here."

Every other man who'd ever taken her home was inside with his belt buckle unfastened by now. Could this guy be for real?

The pressure in Tori's chest built. The pressure that began when she'd agreed to ride to church with Brant.

As they stepped inside the lobby, people greeted them. As a couple. Maybe they shouldn't have come together.

"I wasn't aware our new song director was married?"

An older woman clamped onto Tori's arm. "Where has he been hiding you?"

Song director?

"We're not." Her voice blended with Brant's.

"This is Tori. A friend of a friend. I mean we'll probably end up being friends, but we only met a few days ago."

The older woman's mouth formed an O. "My mistake. But we're glad you came, Tori. Just make yourself at home."

As more people welcomed her, Brant was hustled away by two men in suits. Leaving her alone and outnumbered by people she didn't know. Definitely should have ridden with Jenna and Garrett.

Jenna entered the sanctuary as if on cue followed by Garrett. His presence barely caused a ripple. It was obvious the congregation was used to having the Christian music superstar in their midst.

"I'm so glad you came." Jenna rushed to greet Tori with a hug.

She wished she could say the same, but Tori wasn't glad. She'd never been so uncomfortable in her life.

"Did you meet everyone?"

"And their horse."

"A bit too much." Jenna grimaced. "Let's sit, okay?"

"Yes, please." If Tori could only sink through the floor and disappear. She scanned the church. White walls, soft lighting, burgundy carpet and padded pews. Hymn books in the racks. Not a whole lot different from the church her aunt Loretta attended. The people were just as welcoming. And overwhelming. Why did kindness overwhelm her?

Because she wasn't used to it.

The pianist played a hymn softly as people settled in and the pastor made a few announcements, including the need for a new pianist.

The pianist launched into "Sweet Hour of Prayer" as Brant approached the pulpit. Although she played well, she paid no attention to the timing on the page and set her own pace instead of following the singer. Which was fine, just kept the singer on his toes.

Brant's raspy baritone seemed effortless as he flew threw the song. But from his occasional glances at the pianist, Tori guessed he was being kept alert.

Two more hymns followed and he descended the stage. Her breath caught. Would he sit with her?

Brant glanced at her as he sat by the pastor on the front pew. Something in her stomach balled in a tight knot as the kids dispersed to classes and a man stepped forward to teach.

Stupid. Why had she even thought he might sit with her? What surprised her most was that she wanted him to.

As the deacon wrapped up his lesson, Brant's mind stayed firmly on Tori. He'd have given anything to sit with her. Even with Jenna at her side, she still looked as if she might jump through her own skin. Had she ever been in church before? It hadn't really been a salvation message. And the one thing he knew about Tori for certain, she needed Jesus.

The pastor stood and Brant followed, flipping to the song index as he went. "Have Thine Own Way, Lord." The song that consistently dragged him to the altar even on the rare occasions when he'd been a good boy.

"Turn to page 294." The pianist began playing and thankfully, she kept it slow so the words could hopefully sink into the soul.

On the first verse, a young couple came forward. They'd visited each service consistently in the two weeks he'd been here. Probably considering joining.

Verse two brought a teen girl to the altar. The young

couple stood and a deacon joined them as the pastor's wife knelt at the altar with the girl.

Verse three. The congregation boomed the song—the words written on their hearts. They didn't need him.

Brant stopped singing, descended the stage and knelt at the altar. *Come on, Lord, do your work on Tori. I know she needs you. And if there are any other unsaved souls here, please don't let them leave without your saving grace.* Pressure built in his chest—a physical burden for lost souls.

He stood and found his place in the song. A few more people had come forward. He glanced toward Tori. She was gone. Had she left? No, Jenna was gone, too. He searched the kneeling figures at the altar.

Tori was there. With Jenna by her side.

Chapter 3

Tori's insides would surely explode. "What do I say?" she whispered to Jenna.

"Just tell Him you're sorry for all your sins and you need Him in your life."

All her sins. Could Jesus forgive her for the drinking, the men, the marriage she'd broken up?

"Jesus, I don't know how to do this," she whispered. "I know my life is a mess and I probably deserved Russ's beatings for the bad I've done. I don't want to live like this anymore. Help me."

Some of the ugliness she felt inside seeped away. The roiling in her stomach and pressure in her chest eased. "I don't know if you're real. And if you are, I know I don't deserve your forgiveness. But if you're real, I need you in my life. I need you to fix the mess I've made."

Weak with release, she sagged toward the altar and clutched the wood for support. Words escaped her. But she knew He was real. And He was doing something inside her. Taking all the ugliness out and filling her with something else. Peace. Billowy, soft peace. Strength filled her. Jenna whispered a prayer by her side. And Tori realized the pastor knelt on her other side.

She should stay there for days. It would take months, maybe even years for Jesus to make her clean. But somehow, she knew, He'd already finished. The sins of her entire twenty-eight years had been swept away in just minutes.

Blinking away tears, she turned to the pastor and whispered, "I think I'm a Christian now."

Brant tried to focus on Garrett's conversation, but he'd give anything to be in the office with Tori. Had she accepted Christ? The pastor had closed the service and taken his wife, Jenna and Tori to his office.

"We managed to get a great song director and now in a few weeks, we'll have no pianist." Garrett shook his head. "It's always something."

"Why don't you play for us?" Brant leaned against the end of the pew. "I know you can."

"For the same reason I didn't step into the song director slot. I don't want to distract anyone and I still tour."

At the moment, Brant didn't care if he had a piano player. He could do a cappella. Had before. The only thing that mattered was happening in the office. But he should seem concerned about the pianist situation. "Does anyone else in the congregation play?"

"Two older ladies. But one has arthritis and the other is an in-home caregiver for her mother, so she doesn't always make services. We may have to get you to play your guitar."

"I'm game." Brant glanced toward the office. "What do you think they're doing in there?"

"My guess is Tori's got some questions. Jenna's been witnessing to her for a long time. I hope it took tonight."

"Me, too. Maybe that bully at the store scared her to her knees. How did she end up with a guy like that?"

"Tori's been 'looking for love in all the wrong places' for as long as Jenna's known her."

"I remember that song." Brant snapped his fingers. "It had a happy ending. I hope Tori gets a happy ending. She seems like a nice girl."

"I think she's gonna be okay. Jenna and I will support her in any way we can."

Jenna headed in their direction with Tori close behind. Both ladies wore smiles.

"Tori accepted Jesus." Jenna launched herself into her husband's arms.

"It's about time." Garrett let go of Jenna long enough to hug Tori. "Congrats."

"Thanks." Tori's brilliant smile reached her eyes as she met Brant's gaze.

Should he hug her? Normally, he would welcome a new soul to the fold. But he'd been drawn to Tori from the beginning. Felt protective of her. He hadn't allowed himself to think of a relationship with her because she wasn't a Christian.

But now, she was on equal footing with him in the spiritual realm. Was she ready for a relationship? She'd just come out of an abusive situation. He should probably keep his distance, let her learn who she was in Christ before she got involved with anyone. Why was he even thinking this way?

"Welcome to the family." He gave her a quick, stiff hug.

"Family?"

"Of God." Jenna put an arm around Tori's shoulders. "Once we accept Christ, we're all children of God."

"I've got so much to learn."

"Don't worry. We'll get you a Bible. If you read it and keep coming to church, you'll be amazed at how fast you catch up."

A Bible. Tori didn't have one? How could anyone go through life without a Bible?

He'd have to fix that. It was the least he could do for her.

"Tori?" Jenna's voice tugged her out of her reverie.

"Hmm?" She'd zoned out again with her feather duster frozen in place on a bronze statue. She whisked the duster over the piece.

"You haven't heard a word I've said."

"I'm sorry, what did you say?"

"You'll come to the house for Easter, right?"

"We're not even quite done with February and Easter is early April."

"But you know I plan ahead. So will you come?"

"Thanks, but I'll probably spend Easter with Aunt Loretta."

"Invite her, too. The more the merrier."

The bell above the door rang and Tori whirled around. A woman entered the store.

"May I help you?" Jenna hurried to assist her potential customer.

Even though Russ hadn't made bail yet and Tori had gotten a restraining order against him in case he did, her unease wouldn't go away. She jumped every time the bell above the door rang. Russ would get out. And restraining order or not, he was livid.

While Jenna was busy with the customer, Tori's thoughts went back to running wild with what Russ would do to her. Dusting shelves didn't require enough of her brain.

What had happened to all the peace she had yesterday—her first Sunday morning and evening in church? Less than twenty-four hours later, the real world had intruded. She'd gone to grab lunch and heard three songs about letting your passions rule you. Then, she'd caught a whiff of beer on a cowboy who'd taken the time to look her up and down real slow.

If only she could live at church, maybe this Christian thing could stick. She mentally recited the verse Pastor Thomas had shown her, *But God commendeth his love toward us, in that, while we were yet sinners, Christ died for us.*

The bell rang over the door and she jumped again. A

man entered, but he wore a cowboy hat instead of a ball cap. Not Russ. Great, exactly what she needed. A distraction. She stashed the duster and hurried toward the door. "May I help you?"

Brant. Her steps stalled. Not exactly the distraction she had in mind.

"Um. I happened to be at a Christian bookstore this morning." He cleared his throat. "And I heard Jenna say you didn't have a Bible. So here." He shoved a gift-wrapped book-shaped item toward Tori. Gold ribbon, cream-colored paper with the words *Amazing Grace* in swirled cursive writing.

Gift wrapped? Just happened to be at the Christian bookstore?

Her face warmed as she took the package from him. "Thank you," she mumbled as she untied the ribbon and slid her nail into the taped seam. The paper slid away to reveal a black book with the words *Holy Bible* imprinted in gold.

"Well I knew you needed it now. I mean—you needed it before." Brant winced. "That didn't come out right."

"I did need it. Before and now." She smiled. "My aunt gave me a Bible years ago, but I left it at her house accidentally on purpose."

"Accidentally on purpose, huh?" He chuckled. "I thought I cornered that market."

She ran her hand over the soft, supple cover. Real leather? "I'll treasure it—I mean—I'll read it, too. Thank you."

"You're welcome." He adjusted his cowboy hat. "My church in Pleasant Valley gave new believers a Bible. I'm going to suggest that in Aubrey."

"I'm getting baptized Sunday and joining the church."

"I'm glad."

"I really enjoyed your singing yesterday. You have

a great voice. I play piano." Why had she told him that last bit?

"Really?" His eyebrows went up. "Do you read music?"

"Yes."

"That's awesome. Maybe you could be our new pianist."

She started shaking her head before he even finished the words. "I don't know why I told you that. I can't be the pianist."

"Why? You read music. If you're rusty, I bet a little practice would get you polished up."

"Don't you have to be a preacher's wife? Or have been a Christian for years and years?" Or at least a virgin. All her regrets clogged in her throat.

"Nobody's perfect. Not the preacher. Or the song director. Or the pianist. I think all that's required is the ability to play the piano and a heart that belongs to Jesus."

Tori didn't say anything as she traced the smooth gold lettering with her fingers.

The bell above the door jingled as a customer left.

"Hey, Brant." Jenna joined them.

"He brought me a Bible." Tori cradled the book as if it were treasure. And it was.

Jenna's left eyebrow rose. "Very sweet of him."

"I'm trying to talk Tori into playing piano at church."

"I had no idea she played." Jenna's gaze pinged back to Tori.

"It never came up." Tori shrugged. "And it's been years."

"There's a grand piano and a keyboard at Garrett's sound studio on the ranch and he's not recording for a couple of weeks. Maybe you and Brant can meet there and go over a few songs. See what you got." Jenna turned back to Brant. "You've got the rodeo Friday and Saturday. Got any plans tonight?"

"My sister's birthday is today. I'm having dinner with her. But we'll set up something soon."

"Sure." Tori should protest, but she didn't.

"Sounds good." Brant headed for the door.

Try as she might, she couldn't stop grinning.

The door flew open as Brant knocked and his six-year-old nephew Hunter plowed into him.

"Hey, bud." Brant's heart warmed as he hugged the child. "You're supposed to ask who it is before you answer."

"I seen you out the window."

"Saw." Raquel ruffled Hunter's hair. "Let go of Uncle Brant, so he can come in."

"Happy Birthday, sis." He kissed her cheek and set the gift-wrapped devotional book and that fancy perfume she liked on the coffee table.

"Thanks."

"Smells good." He sniffed the air. Garlic, tomato, cheese. Lasagna. "I'd have gladly taken you out."

"I know. But you know, I love to cook."

"It doesn't seem right cooking your own birthday dinner."

"An excuse to cook all my favorites."

"Lasagna." He waggled his eyebrows.

"I'm gonna get my birthday gift for Mama." Hunter scurried toward his room.

"Anybody else coming?"

"Like who?" Raquel shot him the look.

"Forgive me for hoping you might be seeing someone." He held his hands up in surrender. "What happened to Cody?"

"Cody Warren?" She rolled her eyes. "Mitch forced me into that. I only went out with him twice. And it's been over a year."

"What was wrong with him?"

"He wasn't Dylan."

The sadness in her voice twisted his insides.

"Cody's a nice guy, but we're just friends." Raquel shivered. "He travels the rodeo circuit, riding bulls. If I get involved with someone, it'll be someone who's home every night and has a nice safe job."

Brant wouldn't do it. He would not point out the fact that her Texas Ranger husband died in an off duty car accident. If she was willing to entertain the thought of someone new, and his having a safe job would make her feel better, so be it. Brant just wanted her happy again.

"What about you?" Should have known Raquel would turn the tables on him. "Seeing anyone?"

Not really. But he'd like to.

She zoned in on him. "There is someone."

"A new friend. That's all." For now.

"From the looks of the goofy grin on your face, I'd say she's more than a friend."

"I've only known her a week or so."

"The lasagna comes out in ten minutes." Raquel plopped on the couch and patted the seat beside her. "So, tell me about her."

He sat down. "She's been through a lot—had an abusive boyfriend and just got saved last Wednesday."

"Pretty hefty baggage."

"He's in jail." *My statement helped put him there.* But she didn't need to worry about that.

"That's good."

"I'll have to take things slow. Give her time to heal."

"Time to open presents." Hunter careened into the room holding a misshapen gift covered in wadded wrapping.

Perfect timing. Brant wasn't ready to get into his mixed-up feelings for Tori. Just talking about her pooled his insides. He didn't even know if she'd stick around the church and change her lifestyle for sure. How could a woman he'd met a mere ten days ago draw him like a magnet?

Tori sat at the long table at Moms on Main with damp hair. At least she'd brought a change of clothes for after her baptism. Especially since Jenna had insisted they celebrate it with lunch. No telling what the early March breeze had done to her hair. A week ago, no way would she have gone out to eat with wild hair and running makeup.

But now, peace filled her. And joy put a downright giddiness in her soul. A new start. A new life. A new person. Could God really remake her?

Somehow, she wasn't afraid of Russ anymore. If he came after her, she knew in the end, she'd still be okay.

Aunt Loretta had come for the service and sat beside her now. Jenna approached the table, but left a spot between them. For Garrett? For Brant?

After the service, members of the church had welcomed her with hugs and handshakes. It was all a blur, except for Brant's hug. She could still feel his arms around her. Such gentle strength.

He approached the table. Their eyes met. Her face warmed.

"Here, Brant, you sit here." Jenna gestured to the empty chair between her and Tori. *Lord, help me to focus on You instead of those jade eyes.*

Several other church members lined the table, including Jenna's parents, aunt and uncle, her cousin Caitlyn, and Caitlyn's husband, Mitch. Tori used to feel so uncomfortable around the pristine family, but today it was different. Like she was one of them. Even though Mitch knew way too much about her personal life.

"So, Aunt Loretta, where do you live?" Jenna sipped her tea.

"In Ponder."

"Really?" Jenna peered around Brant at Tori. "I didn't know you had any family near."

"Tori lived with me during her last two years of high school and during design school."

"I need to pick your brain. We met in design school and Tori has worked for me since shortly after we graduated, but she's been very tight-lipped."

Tori hurried to fill the silence. "Aunt Loretta is the only family I have left."

Aunt Loretta's mouth tightened, but she didn't let the tarantula out of its cage. "I'm so glad to know Tori has a church home and good friends. I've worried so over this girl."

"Did Tori invite you to our Easter dinner?"

"No."

"I asked her weeks ago." Jenna shot Tori a look. "Garrett and I would love if you both came to our house after morning services."

So Jenna could pump her aunt for info.

"We could do that." Aunt Loretta sipped her tea. "I'll come the night before and stay at the guesthouse with Tori again."

"Good, it's settled." Jenna clapped her hands.

The food began arriving and thankfully everyone's attention turned to Brant's prayer.

Tori didn't want to get into the subject of her dad. Her upbringing. The violence. Her mom's death. Her stomach took a dive.

No. All that was behind her. She was starting new.

If anyone had told her a month ago that she'd be sitting at a long table in the midst of a church group—after her baptism, no less—she'd have suggested they seek help. She scanned the other tables, the antiques on the walls and a long shelf overhead. Smiles and laughter warmed the room. And she was part of this.

"Hey, you wanna set up an evening next week to get together at Garrett's studio?" Brant's question snapped Tori out of it.

The prayer had ended.

"Sure. What day's good for you?"

"Next Tuesday. Say around six?"

"I don't get off work until six."

"Seven? Eight?"

"Seven will be fine." She scanned the table. Everyone stared at them.

"Tori plays the piano. We're getting together to go over some hymns. She may agree to be our new church pianist."

Aunt Loretta clapped her hands. "Oh that's wonderful. Tori plays beautifully and I always dreamed she'd play for a church someday."

Instead of playing for her dad at his rowdy, beer-splashed concerts. Or at a bar.

Church pianist? A far cry from anywhere she'd ever used her talent before. How had she gotten herself into this?

The sound studio was Nashville worthy, even though the state-of-the-art equipment was in a converted house on Garrett's ranch. Who needed Nashville? But even with the impressive mixing console, massive amps and epic speakers, Brant was more interested in the nervous-looking redhead sitting at the piano.

"Just relax." He shot her a grin. "This isn't an audition. We're two friends having a jam session."

"A jam session?" She swiveled on the piano bench to face him. Her laugh came out harsh. "I've never played hymns in a jam session."

"What have you played?" Maybe talking would relax those stiff shoulders of hers.

"When I was a kid, my mom gave me hymns to practice. But that was years ago. Since then, mostly country." She picked at a loose thread on the corner of the piano bench. "After my mom died, my dad took me on the road with him. He…um…he had a band. I thought he wanted to spend time with me. But it turned out, his keyboard-ist had quit." Her shoulders sagged. "He was using me."

Her stiffness was gone, but defeat threatened.

"Sorry about your mom. I'm sure your dad enjoyed spending time with you while you were his keyboardist."

"My dad is an alcoholic. He doesn't care about any-thing except his next drink and his next woman." Her eyes widened, as if she hadn't meant to reveal so much. "Sorry. TMI alert."

"TMI?"

"Too much information."

"On the contrary, I like learning about you." He just wished she had something good to reveal. Had her whole life been a disaster? "How old were you when you went on the road with him?"

"Sixteen. I only stayed six months. Aunt Loretta didn't think it was a good environment for me, so once Dad found a new keyboardist, she got him to agree to let me stay with her."

Sixteen and playing music with an alcoholic father and his band. Probably in bars and dives. Nowhere a sixteen-year-old girl should be.

"Well, you may not be used to playing hymns, but you read music. Just relax and enjoy playing."

She nodded and turned back toward the piano. Stiff strains of "The Old Rugged Cross" began.

The intro ended and he began singing the words he knew by heart. But he stood behind her as if he needed the hymnal. Or maybe he wanted to be close to her. She'd obviously had it rough and he found himself wanting to sooth her hurts.

As she played the second verse, she visibly relaxed. Her body swayed with her hand movements over the keyboard.

Each note flowed from the piano. He finished the final chorus and applauded.

She turned to face him—as if she were stunned the song was over.

"That's what I'm talking about. You're great, Tori. It was like you became part of the piano. Such beautiful melodies flowed from your fingertips."

"I haven't played like that in years."

"So what do you say, will you play at church?"

She blinked. "I guess. If the congregation is willing to have me."

"We'll have to vote, but I'm certain they'll be as enamored with you as I am."

She blushed and his face heated.

"I mean—enamored with your talent."

But that wasn't all he was enamored with.

Eight o'clock on Saturday night and Tori was in her jammies. Some exciting life she led. But for some reason, she was exhausted.

Smearing cleanser over her face, she wiped her makeup away, then picked up the packet of tiny pills. She poked a pink pill through the foil and popped it in her mouth.

Wait. A. Minute.

She was a Christian now. She'd spent enough time with her aunt and Jenna to know—unmarried Christians didn't take birth control. Unmarried Christians weren't supposed to have sex.

If she was gonna do this, she needed to do it right.

She spat the pill out and washed it down the sink, then punched the remaining two pills through the foil and down the sink.

Wait. A. Minute.

Only three pink pills left. Her breath caught.

She scurried into her bedroom, scanned the calendar and counted the days. When nothing in her life kept a schedule, her cycle did. Like clockwork. Especially when she was on the pill.

Only one other time had she been late. And she'd worried her body into the lapse because she'd forgotten a pill. That time she'd lucked out.

She. Could. Not. Be. Pregnant.

Not with Russ's baby. She sank to the foot of her bed and covered her face in her hands.

"No, Lord. Please. Please, don't let me be pregnant. Not now. Not just when I'm starting to get my life straightened out."

Chapter 4

How long had she sat there staring at the stick? Perched on the side of her bed, Tori glanced at the clock. Eight twenty-seven.

The test she'd bought promised over 99 percent accuracy. Especially if taken first thing in the morning. She'd barely slept last night.

As the dim glow of daylight pierced her curtains, she'd followed the instructions to the letter. Definitely blue. Could it be possible she was the less than 1 percent and the test was wrong?

Of course not. She was Tori Eaton—nothing ever went right in her world.

She dropped the stick and covered her face with both hands.

Why had she thought she could turn her life around? People like her didn't turn their lives around. They just existed between disappointments, delays and defeats.

But she couldn't do this alone. She dialed Jenna's number. Even though they'd been through this last year, Jenna would do it again. And she wouldn't dis Tori in the process.

Garrett Steele crooned a love song in Tori's ear as she waited for Jenna to pick up. Must be nice to have the song your husband wrote for you as your ringtone. At the rate Tori was going, she'd never have a man in her life like that. If she was pregnant Brant would run the other way.

Why had she ever dreamed she could have any kind of future with him?

"Hello?" Jenna's voice was husky.

"Did I wake you?"

"No. I'm getting ready for church. Just haven't had my coffee yet."

"I wouldn't bother you, but—"

"What's wrong?"

"You don't need to pick me up for church. I'm not feeling well."

"Are you sick?" Despite her sleepiness, the worry rang clear in Jenna's tone.

"I've been really tired." Tori closed her eyes. "And I'm late—so I took a home pregnancy test. It's blue."

"I'll be over in a few minutes." No sighing—no judgment. Just Jenna always having her back.

"I can't go, Jenna. I can't face all those people."

"Those people are your church family and all they want is to love you." Stubborn resolve resonated in Jenna's voice. "When you don't feel like going to church, that's when you really need to go. And tomorrow, we'll get you a doctor appointment."

"Do you really think it'll change anything?" Tori stood and paced her bedroom. "It's really blue."

"A professional test never hurts. And if you are pregnant, you'll need prenatal care."

Prenatal care. How could this have happened? An ironic laugh escaped her. She knew how it had happened. If she was pregnant, would the booze and the birth control pills she'd remembered to take hurt the baby?

"Tori, you still there?"

"Yeah, I'm here."

"We'll get through this. No matter what the test says."

Tori's eyes burned. "Jenna…"

"Hmm?"

"Thanks."

"No thanks required. Just hang tight—I'll be over as soon as I'm halfway fit to be seen."

What had she ever done to deserve a friend like Jenna? Nothing.

Spiky blue flowers danced in the spring breeze across the church lot as Brant parked his truck. The phone rang on the seat beside him. He glanced at the caller ID. Raquel?

He grabbed the phone. "You okay?"

"Why do you always think something's wrong when I call?"

"Because you're my little sister and I worry about you."

"Well, I have good news."

"Bring it on." He unbuckled his seatbelt.

"The nurse at Aubrey elementary found out she's pregnant and she's not coming back next year."

"You got the job."

"They called last night. I start in August when the new school year begins."

"That's awesome."

"Do you still think you can get your friend's house?"

"Probably." He gathered his Bible and got out of his truck. "He asked me about it the other day. I'll ask him when I see him this morning at church."

"Well, tell him we'll take it, if you're still in with me. I'm thinking we'll move as soon as Hunter's school wraps up. Mayish?"

"What does Hunter think about moving?" He leaned against the side of his truck bed, enjoying the fresh air.

"He's excited and can't wait to live with his uncle Brant. You sure we won't cramp your bachelor pad?"

"Shoot." He chuckled. "I'm looking forward to having my own personal cook."

"How's it going with the girl you won't tell me about? Does she cook?"

"I honestly don't know. That's how slow it's going. But I think I'm making progress." Several cars pulled in and he checked his watch. "I'll let you know about the house, but I need to get to church now."

"Me, too, we just pulled in. I can't believe how this is falling into place. Dylan and I so wanted to raise Hunter in a small town and give him an upbringing like ours. I wish—"

"He was here." His heart turned over. "Me, too. But you're following his dream and I'll be there. For you and Hunter."

"I know." She sniffed. "I'll talk to you later."

"You okay?"

"Just miss him."

"Me, too."

"I'll talk to you later."

A car parked next to him. He ended the call and peered at the vehicle. Jenna's car. Someone with her. Tori.

He climbed out of his truck. "Morning, ladies."

Tori's eyes were red.

His grin slid from his face. "What's wrong?"

"Nothing." Something unspoken dwelled in Jenna's worried eyes.

"I thought Tori and I might get together at the sound studio again sometime soon since Kate only has a few Sundays left with us."

The breeze caught Tori's hair and she looked like one of those country girls in a music video. She smoothed it in place and hurried ahead of him toward the church.

"Is everything all right?" He gestured toward Tori.

"It will be." Jenna bit her lip.

"Hey is your house still available?"

"Uh-huh."

"Great. My sister and I are interested after all. I'll get with y'all about it soon."

"Sure." Jenna hurried to catch up with Tori.

What was that all about? Just last week, he and Tori had a friendly music session. What had changed since then? Why had she been crying and what kept her from even looking at him now?

Had something happened with Russ?

Tori sat on the white-paper-covered table in the doctor's office. Every fidget resulted in a crinkle and scrunch. Jenna sat in a chair beside her. A repeat. But Jenna hadn't reminded her of last time, she just drove Tori to the doctor. Again.

The waiting was worse than last time. Tori's insides tumbled. "Thanks for coming with me."

"You know, I don't mind." Jenna squeezed her hand.

"I'm sorry." Tori's voice caught.

"Don't, Tori. Like I said, no matter the results, we'll get through this."

"You must be so disappointed." A year ago, they'd been right here. "I didn't learn a thing."

"Yes you did. That happened before. You're different now."

"Am I?"

"Have you gotten drunk since you got saved?"

"No." But it's not like she hadn't thought about it.

"Slept with anyone?"

"No. But give me time. It's only been a few weeks." She moaned. "Why did I think I could turn things around?"

"Because you can. With God's help, you can. Even if you're pregnant."

A tap sounded on the door.

Tori wiped her eyes with the back of her hand. "Come in."

"Ms. Eaton, I have your results." The nurse checked her

laptop. "Congratulations, your results came back positive. You're definitely pregnant."

Her breath froze in her lungs.

"Probably right around four weeks."

She must have gotten pregnant the last week they were together. Maybe even Valentine's Day—the night before she told Russ it was over. The night before that last beating.

Jenna hugged her. "This is wonderful news. A baby. Tori, you're bringing a new life into the world."

"The front desk will give you a schedule of future visits to monitor your pregnancy."

But would the baby be healthy? After so much trauma and mistreatment? "Could I speak with the doctor again? I have a few questions."

"Of course." The nurse slipped out.

"You okay?" Jenna squeezed her hand.

"I'm kind of numb at the moment. And scared."

"You know Garrett and I will support you however we can."

"Yes." Her gaze sank to the floor. "But I'm worried the baby might be hurt."

"Hurt?"

"The last few times I was with Russ—" He'd made her skin crawl. She trembled. "I only slept with him to appease him." Her voice cracked. "To keep him from hurting me. I drank to get through…being with him. I took birth control pills when I wasn't too drunk to remember. And during that last beating, I was already pregnant."

"Oh dear."

Tori picked at the white paper covering the table between her knees until it tore. "Do you think the baby's okay?"

"You need to tell the doctor everything you told me. He'll probably run some tests. But you're a very strong person, Tori. I imagine your baby gets strength from you.

And if anything is wrong, Garrett and I will support you in every way."

Hot tears burned her cheeks. She'd made such a mess of her life. Yet Jenna was willing to help her clean it up.

"Tori?"

"Hmmm."

"Please tell me you plan to continue the pregnancy."

Nausea seized her.

Aunt Loretta's kitchen table—where she'd sought comfort for as long as she could remember. Tori cupped her hands around her coffee mug—hoping the warmth would seep into her bones. Aunt Loretta's tidy house was warm and cozy as usual. But Tori couldn't seem to get warm.

A week spent as an automaton—going through the motions—eating, sleeping, working. Needing to come clean, Tori had stayed here last night. Though she'd worked hard to spare her aunt the ugliness of her life, and often called Jenna when she got herself in a scrape, she'd bared her soul last night. And her aunt had been sympathetic and supportive.

She always felt closer to her mom at Aunt Loretta's. Many times, she and her mom had spent their afternoons here. Her mom bruised and battered with Tori sworn to secrecy and Aunt Loretta clueless to the nightmare they'd lived.

"You better get ready." Aunt Loretta scanned Tori's jammies. "You're up for playing the piano next week. Might look bad if you miss today."

"I don't think I should play the piano at church." Her hands trembled and she almost spilled her coffee. "When I made these plans, I didn't realize I was pregnant."

"Child, this pregnancy happened before you got saved." Aunt Loretta propped her hands on her hips. "And even if it hadn't, Christians are still human."

"So you think I should play for them?"

"I do."

"Do you think I should tell my pastor?"

"For now, you're only filling in. If you feel like you need to, you should tell him. But are you sure you want to let him into a very personal area of your life?"

"I want to come clean." Tori shook her head. No more hiding. Hiding the truth had cost her mom's life. "And eventually, everyone will know anyway."

"I doubt it will make a difference to him. If it does, I'm not sure you've found the right church." Aunt Loretta patted her hand. "Speaking of coming clean—there's one thing you didn't mention last night. What about the father?"

"He beat me up. On several occasions."

Aunt Loretta's breath caught.

"I tried to break up with him, but he got so violent I was scared to leave." She traced her finger around the smooth rim of her mug. "He showed up at Jenna's store, threatened me and broke some lamps. He's in jail and so far he hasn't made bail. Jenna's pressing charges and he'll have a trial at some point."

"You're not still with him?"

"No. That's why I'm staying at Jenna's ranch. I've got a restraining order against him in case he gets out. He doesn't know where I am. Besides, no one can get in the gate without a password or someone in the main house opening the gate."

"You should have come to me." Aunt Loretta smoothed a hand down the length of Tori's hair. "I'd have helped you."

"I didn't want him to hurt you." Tori's voice caught. "And now, since I'm pregnant, I'll be tied to him forever."

"No." Aunt Loretta stomped her foot. "You don't tell him. And don't name him on the birth certificate. A man like that has no rights to an innocent, fragile baby."

"But isn't part of being a Christian being honest?"

"I don't think God expects you to be honest with a man like that. You need to keep yourself and your baby safe."

Tori shook her head and covered her face with her hands. "He'll find out. Even though he's in jail, eventually he'll get out and he'll come after me. I'll get huge and he'll see me."

"We'll keep you safe. I'd like to see this jerk get past me." Aunt Loretta settled in the chair across from Tori, clasping both of her hands. "I'm so proud of you. This baby will complicate everything for you. In an age when women routinely get abortions and kill innocent babies because it's inconvenient, you've decided to keep your child."

"I hope I can do right by this baby." Tori hugged her stomach. "At least I had one good parent to learn from."

"You'll do fine. And I'll be around to help you." Aunt Loretta stood. "Now, you go get ready. And you can talk with the pastor before church."

With leaden legs, Tori stood.

How would her pastor take the news?

And Brant. What would he think of her?

In the principal's office—that's how Tori felt. Only this time, she was in her new pastor's office and she'd just dumped her story at his feet.

A stoic Aunt Loretta sat by her side in front of the oak desk.

"In light of the potential violence from the father," Pastor Thomas cleared his throat, "I think your aunt is right. The fewer people who know about your pregnancy at this stage, the safer you and the baby will be."

The praying hands on the face of the clock on the wall behind the pastor drew her gaze. She read the verse underneath, "And, lo, I am with you always, *even* unto the end of the world. Amen. Matthew 28:20." A comfort. Yet the relentless tick of the clock served as a reminder, she couldn't stop time. Or the progression of her pregnancy.

"But eventually, I won't be able to hide it anymore."

"Maybe by then, the father will be in prison. Did he beat you after you became pregnant?"

She nodded.

Disgust flashed across the pastor's face. "That could help your case. It wasn't just you this man beat up, but an innocent child also."

"I didn't press charges against him. Jenna did because of what he did at her store."

"Why didn't you?"

"Because it would only make him more angry." Tori swallowed hard. "And eventually, he'll get out of jail."

"But the fact that he beat you up during your pregnancy could send him to prison and keep him away from you longer."

"But then he'd know I'm pregnant." Her voice caught.

"Good point." Brother Thomas blew out a frustrated sigh. "How many beatings since the pregnancy?"

Thinking back, she closed her eyes. It had been a month since Russ had beaten her up before that last time. Only because she'd done everything he asked, even stooping to offering sex to appease him. She shivered. "Just once."

"Did you tell your doctor this?"

"Yes. He did an ultrasound and several tests. The baby is fine." Tori's chin trembled. "I can't do anything right. Not even keep a baby safe."

Her aunt patted her knee.

"Tori, you've made some bad choices. But that's in the past." Brother Thomas gave her a reassuring smile. "You're doing the right thing now. The fact that you're continuing your pregnancy is monumental. Under the circumstances, a lot of women would abort."

"And I probably would have a year ago. But not now."

She pressed her hand against her stomach. But should she raise this child? Even if Russ went to prison, eventually he'd get out. And if he learned he had a child, she and her baby would never be free of him. Never be safe.

Besides, what did she know about babies? Surely there were better potential mothers out there looking for a baby. Should she give her baby up?

The pastor checked his watch. "We'd better get to the sanctuary."

"This is Kate's last Sunday, right? Should I still plan to play the piano next Sunday?"

"Yes." Brother Thomas stood. "We usually have a three-month trial period—to make sure a candidate is reliable, can play more than six songs and that no one else is interested—that kind of thing. Then if the candidate is willing, we put it to a vote. When it comes time to vote you in or if you start showing—you'll need to tell the congregation about the baby." He pushed his chair under the desk. "Take a few minutes if you need it."

"I knew he was a good man the first time I met him," Aunt Loretta whispered. "You're in the right church, child."

She'd passed three tests. Jenna, her aunt and her pastor. None had judged her. All supported her.

But how would the congregation feel once they knew the truth?

And more important, how would Brant feel about her?

Something twisted inside her.

Chapter 5

"Tori, would you please come forward?" The pastor gestured toward her.

Brant sent her his best reassuring smile as she stood and made her way to the front of the church, looking shaky.

But she didn't look at Brant. Not even a glance. Just as cold as last week. What was up with her?

"Tori accepted Jesus as her Savior recently, was baptized and joined our church." Clapping echoed through the congregation and the pastor cleared his throat. "And that's not all. Tori plays the piano and has agreed to fill in for us since we're currently musically challenged."

Laughter rippled through the crowd followed by another round of applause as Tori settled at the piano.

"Easter's only a week away." Brant flipped through his songbook. "Maybe next year, we'll have a choir. In the meantime, turn to number 430."

Pages turned and rustled. Would he even be here next year? If he realized his dream of leading music at a megachurch, would he have to read the words off the screen? He loved traditional church. The old hymns, hymnbooks and pews. Surely there was a traditional megachurch out there.

He signaled Tori to begin. Though she still hadn't looked at him, she began playing. Stiff. And she plinked a wrong key twice. Relax. *Lord, help her relax.* She had enough stress in her life. He certainly didn't want to add to it.

Her intro ended and he began singing. Even with her nerves, it was amazing how well their musical styles blended. As if she'd been playing for him their entire lives. She didn't drag him along like the former pianist. Instead, Tori followed his leading. A blessing in a pianist—to know that wherever he went, she'd follow.

As the song continued, she relaxed and her true talent shone. Smiles and nods of approval spread throughout the congregation. From the looks of things—he and Tori would be making beautiful music together for the Lord for a while to come.

Tori had managed to slip away from the Easter dinner at Jenna and Garrett's. Though she'd felt welcome and known most of the people there from church, she had never been to a large family gathering. It had been overwhelming and she was tired.

Early April sunshine warmed her, daffodils nodded in the breeze, robins sang from the live oak trees. But all Tori wanted to do now was go to bed. She entered the guesthouse and made it no farther than the couch, not even sure she had the energy to make it to the bedroom at the moment.

At least Brant hadn't been there. He'd gone to his own family gathering, so she hadn't had to keep him at arm's length all day.

She kicked her shoes off and lay down on the couch, reaching for the faux cowhide throw splayed over the back.

The doorbell rang.

Tori sat straight up, instantly alert.

No one could get past the gate without the password or clearance from the main house.

Yet Tori's heart still clamored. Had Russ found her?

She stood and started for the door, then pressed herself against a wall. Silently, she tiptoed to the foyer, careful not to creak any floorboards or bump anything, and peered through the peephole.

Jenna. With another woman. She looked like Jenna's cousin, Caitlyn—only older. Aunt Millie.

Tori undid the locks and swung the door open.

"Hey." Jenna gave her a quick hug, ushered the older woman in and shut the door. "You know Natalie and Caitlyn's Aunt Millie."

"It's nice to officially meet you."

"You, too." Millie smiled. "I saw you at lunch and I've seen you at church, but I've never gotten the chance to speak to you other than in passing." Aunt Millie fidgeted. "I told Jenna we should call first. Maybe I should wait in the car."

"No." Jenna grabbed Millie's arm. "I want you to talk to Tori."

"About what?" The adrenalin over an unexpected guest drained away and once again all Tori wanted was her bed.

"Have you thought about pressing charges against Russ?"

Tori trembled. Did Millie really need to hear this? "To be honest. No. Maybe if I leave things as is, he'll leave me alone. If I press charges, he'll want revenge."

"I'd like you to talk to Millie."

Tori searched her memory. "Are you a shrink or something?"

"Heavens no." Millie smiled but it soon slid from her mouth. "I lived with an abusive husband for several years. Jenna thinks hearing my story might help you."

"I don't see how."

"Just humor me." Jenna clasped her hands as if in prayer.

"I told Jenna we should call and set this up. We can talk another time."

Tori knew Jenna well enough to know—she might as well do it and get it over with. "Now is fine."

"Great." Jenna shot her a triumphant smile. "I'll go on to the house and let y'all talk. And I really appreciate you doing this, Millie."

"No problem. I hope it helps." Millie's gaze caught Tori's.

The door shut behind Jenna and Tori tried not to squirm.

"I can see Jenna's decorating touch here. A bit rustic, but the creamy walls and drapery are all Jenna."

"It's amazing how much you look like Caitlyn."

"So I've been told."

"So tell me again, why aren't you Jenna's aunt, too?" Tori already knew, but she was desperate to avoid the coming conversation.

"Natalie and Caitlyn's mother is my sister. Jenna is related to my nieces on her dad's side."

"Oh." It didn't happen often, but Tori didn't know what to say. Smack dab out of small talk and she did not want to have this discussion.

"I hear you have a problem with a man in your life."

"That's a delicate way to put it." Tori hugged herself. "Please, sit down. Would you like some sweet tea? Water?"

"No thank you." Millie settled on the white leather sofa. "He's in jail?"

"Yes. And in case he manages to come up with bail, Jenna helped me get a restraining order against him." Tori chose her favorite wingback and stared at the taxidermied longhorn head over the Austin Stone fireplace. Totally not Jenna. But it fit Garrett.

"I met Stuart at the rodeo." Millie's hands shook and she clasped them in her lap. "I was sixteen, he was twenty-one. I knew my parents would have a cow about him, so I kept our romance secret."

"You don't have to tell me all of this." Tori held her hands up as if warding off a blow. "I'll let on to Jenna that we had a good talk without you having to spill your guts to a complete stranger."

"It's okay. I've been sharing my story at battered women's shelters, hoping it can help someone else." Millie tucked her hair behind her ear. "Stuart was really sweet at first, but the more I saw him, he became jealous and controlling. By the time he actually hit me, I was already afraid to break up with him."

The story of Tori's life with Russ. Of her mom's story with Tori's dad. She clutched a cowhide throw pillow against her stomach.

"He wanted me to run away with him and all I wanted to do was run away from him. But the slapping about turned into full-out beatings and I found myself doing whatever he wanted, whatever I could to placate him so he wouldn't hurt me." Millie's gaze dropped to her hands.

"But it didn't matter. No matter how easygoing I was, he beat me. He'd go off without warning, yet he was always careful not leave any marks I couldn't cover up with clothing. He threatened to harm my family if I didn't run away with him, and I didn't see any other choice, so I went with him."

If Caitlyn and Natalie's family was a reflection of Millie's family, she'd had a strong unit. People she could turn to, but she hadn't. Just like Tori's mom hadn't turned to Aunt Loretta. And Tori hadn't turned to her aunt. Or Jenna.

"I didn't want to bring a child into such a violent situation, so I managed to sneak off and get birth control." Millie's voice trembled. "But a few years later, he found the pills and...well that time, I ended up in the hospital."

"The doctor—the nurses—they had to have known what happened to you."

"They did." Millie nodded, her gaze never leaving the

floor. "But I was afraid he'd go after my parents or my sister. I told them I fell off a ladder. Our son was born a year later and thank goodness Stuart never turned on Trent.

"But as Trent got older, I knew it wasn't a good thing for him to see his mother get beat up all the time. Neighbors called the police on several occasions, but I said I fell down the stairs or ran into the cabinet or tripped over a toy."

The same stories Tori's mom had told. "My dad wasn't home much—but when he was—he beat my mom. She always denied he'd done it and swore me to secrecy."

"And it scarred you. That's probably how you got mixed up with an abusive boyfriend. It becomes a way of life." Millie's gaze met Tori's. "But I didn't want that for Trent. I tried to take him and leave twice. But each time, Stuart found us. And each time, the beating was worse. Finally, I decided that if I left—without Trent…"

A sob escaped Millie and Tori handed her a tissue box. "I thought if I left, he wouldn't come after me as long as he had Trent and the violence would stop. And it worked, I got away.

"I'd learned how to make fake ID's from him and started over in a different state." Millie dabbed her eyes. "But I never forgot my son. I subscribed to the paper here and watched the obituaries—hoping to see Stuart's so I could come home.

"I finally got my wish—there it was—Stuart's obituary." Millie's chin trembled and she held a crumpled tissue to her mouth. "I came home and contacted my family. I found my son. But he hated me because after I left, Stuart took his frustrations out on Trent. He even put him in the hospital once."

Tori closed her eyes.

"Trent testified against him, but by then he was eighteen and Stuart only got a year in jail." Millie straightened her shoulders. "After he got out, he saw Caitlyn at the rodeo. I don't know if it was the alcohol or what, but by then I guess his brain wasn't firing right. He thought Caitlyn was me and he started writing her these creepy, threatening letters."

"Like a stalker?"

"Yes, but he didn't stop there. She was leaving her store one night and he attacked her." Millie dabbed her eyes. "With a knife—stabbed her twice. But she managed to get away."

"I remember hearing about an attack a few years ago, but I never knew it was Caitlyn." A chill ran up Tori's spine. "Jenna never let on. I remember her being jumpy, but I thought it was because of an attack so close to home."

"Very close to home."

"So what happened with Stuart?"

"Caitlyn went into protective custody. Texas Rangers lured Stuart out of hiding, but he got away. When they caught up with him again, he killed himself."

"And you got to come home to your son."

"We've spent the last few years rebuilding our relationship." Millie sniffled. "It was hard. Trent had a lot to forgive me for and I had to forgive myself. I'm still working on that, but we're getting there. And I became a Christian last year, so that's helped with the forgiveness part."

"I guess Jenna wanted you to tell me all of this in hopes of convincing me to press charges." But hearing Millie's story only frightened her more.

"You should press charges, Tori."

"But even if I do, he'll get out." Tori shook her head. "Way too quick. Like Stuart. Trent pressed charges and Stuart was out a year later to wreak havoc on Caitlyn."

"True. But don't you see." Millie closed her eyes. "If I had pressed charges all those years ago, maybe Stuart wouldn't have hurt Trent. Or Caitlyn. Or in the end, himself. My silence cost me my son, gave Trent broken bones and years of terror, wounded my niece, stole her peace of mind and robbed my son of a father."

"I'm pregnant." Tori's shoulders slumped.

"With your abuser's baby? Oh you poor child."

"I'm thinking about giving the baby up, so Russ won't ever hurt him or her."

"You shouldn't have to give your baby up to keep him or her safe." Millie's tone pleaded. "Press charges. Maybe he'll get prison time and counseling. And it could turn him around. Maybe you can keep your baby. And maybe you can save other people from this man."

If Tori did nothing, even if he left her alone and she could keep the baby's existence from him, he'd move on to some other victim. And it would be Tori's fault.

"Please don't tell anyone about my pregnancy. I'm trying to keep it quiet as long as I can, so hopefully Russ won't find out."

"Of course. Sorry to dump my guts all over your living room. Along with some emotions thrown in." Millie blew her nose. "I'll leave you alone to think about what I've said."

"I appreciate you coming. Being so honest and sharing your life with me when you don't even know me."

"I hope hearing my story helps you." Millie stood. "I can tell you're getting your life on the right track."

"I hope so." Tori stood and hurried to open the door for Millie.

Millie stopped at the door and turned to face Tori. "I recently learned that Trent fathered a child as a teen and the baby was given up for adoption. I've gotten acquainted with my granddaughter."

"I'm glad you got things worked out with your family."

"Me, too. But the reason I told you that—I know you

don't feel like you could ever possibly trust another man right now. But don't let Russ close your heart."

She'd already met a man she could trust and her heart definitely wasn't closed toward him. It was just too late.

"Through getting to know my granddaughter, I met her adoptive grandfather." Millie blushed. "He's a pastor, widowed for years. At first, I wanted nothing to do with him. But, he's the most considerate and tender man I've ever known. God sent the perfect balm to heal all my wounds. We're getting married next month."

"That's awesome!"

"It is." Millie's smile went soul deep. "God took all my mistakes and patched them together. I thought I'd never be happy again. He can do the same for you. Keep your heart open and when God sends you the right man, you'll know it."

Heat crept up Tori's neck. She opened her mouth, but nothing came out.

He already had. Brant was the kindest, gentlest man she'd ever known. But God's timing was off on this one. Russ still lurked in the background. And his baby grew in her belly. Even if Brant were willing to take that on, she wouldn't let him. He deserved better.

Finally Saturday. Brant had looked forward to meeting Tori at the sound studio all week. Early May and he'd barely seen her outside of church for the last month. Maybe he'd start singing more solos so they'd need to practice more often.

Sorry, Lord. Concentrate on singing for the Lord. Not seeing Tori.

He pulled in at the sound studio, grabbed the McDonald's bag and got out of his truck. No sign of her yet.

He let himself in and set her food on the bar at the kitchen counter. Gravel crunched outside and a car door slammed. Should have brought candles and a vase with a rose. And saved his food to eat with her. He needed to work on his win-the-girl skills.

The door opened and she stepped inside. "Hey."

"Hey." Should have opened the door for her. "I had to run an errand in Denton, so I brought you lunch. Have you eaten yet?"

"No. I could use some comfort food. I really appreciate this." She rewarded him with a smile and headed straight for the counter. But as she opened the Filet-O-Fish box, all color drained from her face. Her hand flew to her mouth and she scurried from the room.

"Tori?" Brant hurried after her. What had he done to upset her?

She charged into the bathroom and slammed the door in his face.

Heaves echoed through the wooden door. "Tori. Are you all right? Can I come in?"

"I'm fine." But more heaves followed her words.

"I'm coming in." He opened the door.

She knelt at the toilet holding her hair back with one hand as a spasm hit her.

"Why didn't you tell me you were sick?" He hurried to her and held her hair for her.

Soft and silky as he'd imagined. How could he find her so beautiful while she puked her guts out?

He'd always had a strong stomach, but he must have a thing for women throwing up. Memories rushed over him. The same situation. Only with Tiffany—his first love—holding her hair back while she tossed her cookies.

He must be one sick puppy. Lovesick puppy.

Love? Tori? Sure he was attracted to her. But had it become more than that?

She finished, flushed the toilet and slumped against the wall beside her.

Brant grabbed a washcloth out of a froufrou basket by the sink, ran cool water over it and handed it to her.

She wiped her mouth—pale and weak. "Sorry about that. You shouldn't have come in here with me."

"How long have you been sick?"

"I'm fine." She pushed to her feet. "And I'm not really sick."

"Could have fooled me. It's still flu season, you know." Brant caught her elbow, but she didn't seem wobbly.

"I'm pretty sure it's not that. But you might keep your distance just in case." She pulled away from him and walked back to the kitchen with no problem.

"I'll put the food in the fridge."

"No, I'd like to eat now. I'm starving."

Something in Brant's gut shifted. He'd known of two women who'd lost everything their insides consisted of and then immediately been hungry. Tiffany and Raquel. And they'd both been...

"You're pregnant?"

Chapter 6

Tori's hand went to her stomach. "How did you know?"

"Because I've been there before." Twice. "With my… sister. Raquel used to throw up and then be hungry right afterward."

"Please don't tell anyone." She covered her face with her hands.

"Of course not. It's not my place. How far along are you?"

"About ten weeks. It's Russ's baby and I don't want him to know."

Brant did a quick count in his mind. His heart clenched. "You were pregnant when he beat you up."

"Yes. But I told the doctor. He ran tests. The baby's fine."

The tightness in his chest eased up. "Do you know if it's a boy or girl?"

"Wrong position when they did the ultrasound. They couldn't tell."

"When is Russ's trial? You'll start showing at some point."

"Next month. I'm hoping I won't be showing by then and can testify against him." She closed her eyes. "And I'm not trying to be dishonest with the church. Pastor Thomas knows. He thought I should keep Russ from knowing and that's why I haven't told the congregation yet—to keep my pregnancy quiet. But I plan to tell them before the vote."

"What can I do to help?"

"Nothing. It's just a mess." Tears welled in her eyes and one traced down her cheek.

The boundary breaker. He stepped closer and pulled her into his arms.

She started shaking and soft sobs turned into a meltdown on his shoulder. Despite her distress, all he could think about was how good it felt to hold her like this.

After a few minutes, she quieted. And pulled away from him.

She was good at that.

He handed her a McDonald's napkin and she dabbed her eyes.

"Let me eat and freshen up and I'll be ready." Some strength came back into her tone as she perched on a stool at the bar. "I guess you're not hungry?"

"I ate on the drive over." He settled on a stool beside her.

"I'm glad. You probably would have lost your appetite by now. You watched me puke and then I sobbed all over you."

"Actually, I've always had a strong stomach." And she was still beautiful. As he admired her beauty, he could imagine her pregnant—huge with Russ's child. And it wouldn't change a thing about the way he felt about her.

What was wrong with him? How many men had a thing for a puking woman pregnant with another man's child?

With Tiffany, he'd been in love with her long before he'd known about her baby. And the same with Tori. His feelings had been developing for her from the moment she'd threatened him with the poker. He seemed to be destined to find the perfect woman after she'd been used and dumped by some jerk.

At least Tori wouldn't do what Tiffany had. Tori was stronger.

Tori popped the last bite of the sandwich in her mouth,

followed it with her last three fries and took a long drink of her shake. Wow, she'd eaten fast. But her stomach had definitely been empty and she was eating for two. If he'd known that before, he'd have gotten her vegetables or something.

"I wish I'd brought you something more nutritious."

"It was perfect."

"You need to eat healthy. For the baby. Once we get settled in the new house, I'll have Rock fix you a good meal."

"Rock?" Her puzzled frown was cute. Who was he kidding? Anything she did looked cute to him.

"My sister, Raquel. I call her Rock. Anyway, she doesn't know anybody here. I'd like her to make some friends and she loves to cook."

"We'll see. Um, we'd better get to work."

Could he step in and fix the holes Russ had created in her heart? In her life? In her child's life?

His heart wanted to run before it could get hurt again. But surely history wouldn't repeat itself. He couldn't lose her, too. He just couldn't. He'd see to it.

He'd support Tori. And love her. That he could do—without even thinking.

The end table wasn't heavy, just bulky as Brant maneuvered it through the door of Jenna's house. No, it was his and Rock's now. Mid-May's breezy sunshine was perfect for moving a few things Raquel and Hunter could do without in Garland until school wrapped up.

"Oh, be careful," Raquel called behind him. "You're gonna hurt your back."

"I told you, it's not heavy." He was more worried about scuffing the table.

He set the table down and turned to see Hunter struggling to carry a box bigger than he was with the word *books* written in Sharpie across the top. "Need help, bud?"

"I got it." The six-year-old voice sounded strained.

Every instinct in him wanted to scoop the heavy box out of his nephew's arms. But Hunter wanted to help and Brant wouldn't steal his thunder. "Just set it down if you need to. Rest a bit and then take it on into the den. Or you can go get another box and I'll take it to the den."

Hunter set it down and Brant patted him on the shoulder. "Good job, bud."

His cell phone rang and he dug it out of his pocket. "Hello?"

"Hey, Brant, it's Jenna. I need help with Tori."

His heart jumped. "Is something wrong?"

"No. In fact, it's great. Tori's agreed to press charges against Russ. But I'm afraid if she waits 'til after work to file a report, she'll back out."

"I'd love to see Russ in jail, but isn't it a bit late for pressing charges?"

"Probably, but I called Mitch. He said the charges may not stick, but at least they'll be on file."

"What can I do?"

"Mitch is actually in forensics, but he was in the area the day Russ came to my store. He's ready to take Tori's statement."

He scanned the house with boxes and Raquel's furnishings scattered about. This could wait. "I can take her to his office."

"Could you? I know you're moving, but I'm so afraid she'll change her mind."

"I'll be right over. Is she at the store?"

"No, she was distracted, so I sent her home. I was hoping I could get one of my other employees to cover for me, so I could take her, but it's not working out."

"I'm on it."

"Thanks, Brant."

He'd do whatever he had to do to help insure that monster never touched Tori again.

Raquel shuffled in the door with a box marked *shoes*.

"Hey, Rock, what do you say, we take a break?"

"I'm fine. You can take one if you need to."

"I actually need to run an errand and it could take a while." He ruffled Hunter's hair. "And I don't want to worry about you two strapping specimens hurting yourselves while I'm gone."

"We'll be fine."

"How about y'all stay busy unpacking boxes and leave the heavy stuff alone until I get back? Promise?"

"Promise." Raquel and Hunter's voices mingled as they both gave him a Boy Scout salute.

"You really didn't have to drive me." The quiver in Tori's voice contrasted her words. "I don't mind."

She'd been mostly quiet during their drive to Garland, but at least she'd agreed to come. He remembered the last time she'd been in his truck. After Russ's little performance at the store, when she'd been shaken and skittish.

Much the same way today. And she was always skittish, where he was concerned anyway. Though she'd consistently shown up at church and played piano for him for a month and a half, he hadn't gotten her to agree to practice anymore.

The only time they'd been alone was that session at the recording studio. Until today.

"I should have pulled up my big girl boots and driven myself."

"Will you stop. I said I don't mind. Want to swing through McDonald's first? Maybe some comfort food would help." The last time he'd tried to feed her hadn't gone well. "But maybe on second thought…"

That got a grin out of her. "I'm usually okay this time of day. Maybe afterward."

"Suits me." He found a parking slot at the Ranger Company "B" Headquarters. "Ready?"

She looked small. And scared. "No."

More than anything, he wanted to pull her into his arms, offer her comfort, strength, and his heart. How could he have such feelings for her when he'd only known her three months?

"You're supposed to be moving. Why did Jenna call you?"

"None of the other employees could cover for her at the store. I figure if Garrett went with you, that would mean publicity. And I'm the only other witness to the injuries Russ gave you." His jaw clenched at the memory of her battered, but still beautiful face the first night he'd met her.

"I guess Jenna's afraid I'll change my mind about pressing charges. But I won't. I'm prepared to do whatever it takes to keep Russ away from this baby. But you need to get back to moving and I can get a taxi home."

"No need. I'm fine. I'll wait." He got out, went around and opened her door.

She made no move to get out of the truck.

"Want me to go with you?"

"Would you?"

"I'll even hold your hand if you want."

She blew out a big breath. "I might take you up on that."

"What are you waiting for?" He offered his hand.

Uncertainty mirrored in the blue-gray depths of her eyes as her gaze met his—then dropped to his hand. She placed her trembling fingers in his and he held on as she climbed down from his truck.

He didn't let go as they walked toward the building that housed Mitch's office. And she didn't pull away.

* * *

"So your relationship with Russ Dawson lasted six weeks?" Mitch typed on his laptop.

"Yes." If you could call what they'd had a relationship. With each click of Mitch's fingers over the keys, Tori had second thoughts. About pressing charges and about asking Brant to stay with her in Mitch's office. Did she really want him hearing all of this?

"During those six weeks, how many times did he beat you up?"

"Four times." Her insides twisted.

"Did you see a doctor? Or file a report with the police any of those times?"

"No."

"Any pictures of injuries?" Mitch's fingers stopped moving.

"No."

"Any witnesses?"

"No."

Mitch looked at her over the laptop, then closed it. "I feel for you, Tori. My blood boils when I think of a man hitting a woman, but with no evidence—I have to be honest, the charges probably won't stick."

"But I can testify." Brant jumped up as if ready for battle.

What had she ever done to deserve him? He knew the truth now. He knew they could have no future. Yet, he was still at her side.

"Did you see him hit her?" Mitch's attention turned to Brant.

"No. But I saw the aftermath. Her eye was so swollen she couldn't even open it and her lips were cut. She had a black eye for a week."

"And how do you know Russ Dawson caused that?"

"Tori told me."

Mitch shook his head. "That's not enough. I wish it was, but it's not."

"Garrett and Jenna saw her after that last beating, too."

"But they didn't see Russ hit her?"

"No." Brant deflated. "But I can testify that he threatened her at Jenna's store. And all of the cowboys who came to the rescue that day are willing to testify. I saw her after the beating and we all saw Russ at the store." Brant's tone heated. "He had Tori cornered with that piece of glass in his hand."

"I really don't think we'll be able to make anything stick except the incident at the store. We have witnesses to the actual event in that case."

"So, you're saying I shouldn't bother?" Tori's voice came out small, frightened. She straightened her shoulders.

"No. You should definitely press charges. Even if they don't stick, it'll be on his record. Then if he hits someone else someday, your charges will show a pattern. Maybe make charges stick next time."

"You think there'll be a next time?" She clasped a hand to her mouth.

"That day in the store, I thought Russ looked familiar. I finally remembered, I had a run-in with him a few years back on a stakeout."

"And?" Hope echoed in Brant's tone.

"Let's just say Russ is a textbook case. Men like this don't usually stop abusing. They move on to their next victim."

"I think you should tell him the rest, Tori."

Her mouth opened, but nothing came out. She shot Brant the evil eye.

Mitch caught her gaze. "Is something else?"

"I'm—" Tori squeezed her eyes closed. "I'm pregnant."

"With Russ's child?" Mitch's eyebrows rose, but his expression showed no judgment.

"Yes."

"Were you pregnant during any of the beatings?"

"The last one." She shook her head. "The first three beatings happened in the first two weeks we were together. Then there was a span of time he didn't hit me—I'd learned to be very acquiescent and keep him calm. Until I tried to break up with him. I learned a month later that I was a month pregnant."

"That could change your entire case." Mitch leaned toward her. "Even without proof of any of the beatings, with Jenna testifying about the incident at the store and the men backing her up with their account of seeing Russ corner you. We might have something."

"I don't want Russ to know about the baby." If she could keep Russ in the dark, maybe she could keep her baby and they could have a normal life. But it could never work. The only way to keep him in the dark would be to give the baby up. She wasn't sure if she had enough strength to do it.

"Completely understandable. Men like Russ have no right getting near a child. But—" Mitch sat back in his chair. "I'm afraid without revealing your pregnancy, we're back to square one."

Tori huffed out a sigh. "I'd like to press charges without revealing my pregnancy. Even if Russ doesn't get much jail time, at least it'll be on his record."

"All right." Mitch opened his laptop again.

Something touched the back of her hand. Tori looked down. Beside her, Brant offered his hand. She clasped onto the lifeline he offered, needing all the strength she could get.

The pastor ended the altar call after the half dozen who'd gone forward—including Tori—returned to their seats. Thank goodness, this church allowed the pianist altar time, too. All she'd had to do was signal the sound booth. He'd started a CD right where she'd left off and she'd gotten some much needed strength through prayer.

"Now Tori has something she'd like to share with us." Pastor Thomas motioned for her to come stand beside him in front of the pulpit.

As she took her place, she noticed movement from behind her. Brant stood on her opposite side and took her hand in his. Jenna and Garrett stood amongst the congregation and came forward to stand behind her.

Tori's eyes misted. She'd told them today was confession day for her, but she hadn't expected this show of support. She blinked several times and cleared her throat.

"I haven't been a Christian for long and I've made lots of mistakes in the past." Her voice quivered. "And as we all know, mistakes have consequences. So as a result of mistakes I made before I discovered Christ, I'm pregnant."

Chapter 7

The congregation grew so quiet and still, she could have heard a feather drop. Brant squeezed her hand.

"Tori came to me with this news a few months ago." Pastor Thomas took over for her. "She thought she shouldn't play the piano because of her pregnancy. But I convinced her otherwise. She wanted to come forward then, but I advised her not to."

Tori summoned up all the strength she had. "I found out about the baby right after I joined this church. But the baby's father is very abusive and I don't want him to know about my pregnancy. So Pastor Thomas advised I keep quiet. The father ended up in jail not long after I broke up with him and he has an upcoming trial. We were hoping the trial would be over by now." Would he always haunt her?

Every eye was on her, but try as she might, she couldn't read the congregation. "But I'm right at three months now and I'm starting to show. Plus the vote is coming up and I wanted everyone to know the truth. In fact, I've felt like a terrible liar by not telling you."

Brant squeezed her hand again and she could have hugged him at that moment. A hand settled on each of her shoulders. Jenna and Garrett lending their support. Tears filled her eyes.

"We need to support Tori." Pastor Thomas paused a moment, letting the words sink in. "She could have easily aborted this unplanned pregnancy. This child certainly complicates her life by tying her to a man she does not want to be tied to. But she's doing the right thing by her child."

The child. Tori had to stop thinking of the baby as hers. It was the only way she could truly do the right thing and give the baby up.

A smattering of applause started up in the back corner of the congregation. Then it spread until everyone was clapping. Approving her decision to keep the baby. The tears welling in her eyes spilled as people began standing until the entire congregation stood. Her friends surrounding her joined in the applause.

Her first standing ovation. Probably her only one. She dabbed at her eyes.

"Wonderful." Pastor Thomas joined the applause, but stopped long enough to press a tissue into her hand, then waited until the clapping died down. "I ask that everyone continue to support Tori and keep her secret. She doesn't need a violent man in her life. Or in her baby's life."

The pastor dismissed with a prayer. Jenna hugged her, then Garrett, and Brant. His was a nice long hug and she could have stayed there forever. But other people came forward to offer their support and he had to turn her lose. Soon she was lost in a sea of hugs from people whose names she hadn't even learned yet.

Tori sagged into each embrace. The stress of keeping her secret and relief it was out in the open now physically weakened her.

Thank you, God, for bringing me to this church.

Brant opened the door of Garrett's sound studio. Tori spun around.

"Relax. It's me." Brant held his hands up in surrender. "Please don't get your poker."

That almost got a smile out of her. "Hey."

Almost. How could he forget? She'd probably be jumpy for years after her debacle with Russ. His blood boiled. What he'd like to do to that jerk. He'd have to remember not to sneak up on her in the future. "Anything in particular you'd like to play first? A favorite? Something you're comfortable with?"

A bitter laugh escaped her. "I'm comfortable with honky-tonk, but that doesn't fit at church."

"Tell me about your dad's band."

"It's a long story." She trailed her fingers lightly across the glossy ivory keys.

"It's kind of stuffy in here—actually cooler outside. What do you say we sit outside a bit while the air conditioner kicks in."

"I can't play piano outside."

"No, but I'm singing a solo with my guitar. I can practice that and you can give me feedback."

"I was just thinking how nice it would be to while away an afternoon in that tree swing around the side of the house." A dreamy expression settled on her face. "I never had a swing when I was a kid."

"Never? The afternoon's waiting." Brant opened the door. "June will be here before you know it and it'll be too hot to while away anything outside."

"I wish spring lasted longer." Tori hurried past him leaving a trail of her flowery scent.

Brant followed her out, then walked to his truck to gather himself. And his guitar. By the time he rounded the house, Tori was swinging high. Her hair trailed behind her and a wide smile curved her beautiful lips.

He settled at the base of the huge live oak tree and strummed his guitar, wanting to sing her some sappy love song. Instead, he concentrated until he remembered the words—"How Great Thou Art." Yes, concentrate on God.

Not Tori. He lost himself in the song—losing all sense of time and place.

As the song wrapped up, he repeated the final chorus.

Applause brought him back with a thud. Tori sat in the still swing, clapping.

He cleared his throat. "You could accompany on the piano if you want."

"No. It's perfect. Just like that." She stood and walked toward him. "I always wanted to play guitar. Could you teach me?"

"Sure." He stood, pulled the guitar strap loose and handed it to her. "You already know music, so you're ahead of the game."

"Show me the chords."

Brant stood to her left and positioned her fingers on the strings. Then moved to her right to position her other hand. There was just no way to do this other than stand behind her with his arms sort of around her.

With each of his hands on hers, his chest against her back, he helped her strum. But something was off-kilter other than his heartbeat. What emanated from the guitar sounded nothing like the simple bar chord he'd planned.

She laughed back over her shoulder at him.

And his gaze settled on her lips, then bounced back up to meet her eyes. "Um, let's try again. It's really easy."

"No." She pushed the guitar away and slipped out of his arms. "We're here to practice with the piano. Better get to it."

What was that?

"Tell me about you." Tori managed to keep her voice steady despite her rocketing heart, as she settled back at the massive grand piano. "You met Garrett in Nashville, but now you're here in a small church in Aubrey."

"Chasing a dream. A new dream." He closed his eyes.

"I only gave myself a year in Nashville. When I didn't get my big break in that year, I gave up that dream and found a new one. I want to be the music minister at a megachurch someday." He pressed his fingers to his lips. "Shhhh. Don't tell the church that."

And her gaze stayed on his lips for a beat. They'd been so close to hers. So inviting. Why did the only nice, un-attached man she'd ever met have to be a musician? And why did she have to meet him when she was pregnant?

Mental shake back to the conversation. What were they talking about? Oh yeah, his dream. "And you think our church will do that for you?"

"No. But being the headliner at the Fort Worth Stock-yards Championship Rodeo might."

"Oh, I see."

"I came to our church because they happened to need a song director." He propped his booted foot on the rung of her bench. "Your turn—tell me something about Tori Eaton. Starting with telling me about your dad's band."

A huge sigh escaped her. Might as well get it out in the open. "Ever heard of Slim Easton?"

Recognition dawned in Brant's eyes. "Sure, the coun-try star."

"His manager thought Easton had more star power than Eaton. He's my dad." Her shoulders slumped. "He cheated on my mom and was never home. When he did come home, he spent his time beating my mom up." Her words came out matter-of-factly—as if her dad's cheating and beating were a normal part of everyday life.

"I'm so sorry." There was nothing matter-of-fact about the compassion in Brant's tone.

"Mom tried to make the best of it." She shrugged. "After he beat her, I'd tend her wounds. And as soon as he left—" and she could walk straight "—she'd take me to McDon-ald's for comfort food—Filet-O-Fish, fries and a chocolate milk shake. She'd tell me how stressed my dad was and that one day his music wouldn't stress him out so much and he'd stop hitting her."

Brant's hand settled on her arm. "You don't have to tell me any more. I had no idea."

The warmth and gentleness of his touch gave her strength.

"No, it feels kind of good to talk about it. I've never told anyone. Not even Aunt Loretta or Jenna." She swiped at her eyes. "When I was fifteen. He beat her up really bad—worse than ever before. I tried to take care of her, but she needed a doctor and I wanted to stay home from school with her. She insisted I go and I made her promise we'd see a doctor after school. When I came home that day, I found her in the tub. She'd slashed her wrists."

"Oh, Tori." Brant settled on the bench beside her and his arms came around her. The solidness of his chest cushioned her cheek. The first man capable of a tender embrace to cross her radar screen. She could get used to it.

"My dad took me on the road with him." She mumbled against his shoulder.

"I'm so sorry you had to grow up that way. It explains a lot."

"Like how I ended up with Russ." She shrugged. "Habit, I guess."

"Did your dad ever hurt you?"

"Not physically." She really should scoot away from the song leader, but her scooter wouldn't obey. "I fantasized that things would be different on the road—we'd develop a normal father/daughter relationship, he'd be kind and we'd spend time together."

The only time she'd gotten any attention from her father during that six months was when he'd caught her consoling herself in his drummer, Kenny's bed. She winced as the things he'd called her echoed from the past.

Her laugh echoed irony. "But I soon learned he only took me with him because his keyboardist quit after he found out Dad had an affair with his wife. And Dad didn't have time for me. He only cared about his booze and his groupies."

Brant's fingers stroked soothing circles on her back.

"I'm sorry, Tori. That sounds lame, but I'm really sorry."

"I survived." She tried to sound as if none of it mattered. "After six months, he sent me home to live with Aunt Loretta. I graduated, went to design school and met Jenna."

"And landed your dream job."

"Not exactly. Don't get me wrong, I like working with Jenna and she's been better than wonderful to me. But I went to design school to study clothing design."

Even with the good influence of Aunt Loretta and Jenna, she'd followed a destructive path. She'd set out to punish every musician she met—to the point of telling Rick's wife about their affair and trashing his marriage last year. But during all those years, all those relationships, she'd only ended up hurting herself.

And here she was pregnant by an abusive musician, and accepting comfort—from a musician. She pulled away from Brant and moved away from him on the bench.

"I met Russ in a dive—he was playing guitar for some two-bit country band. But you know, maybe meeting him was a good thing." Except for his child growing in her belly. The baby wasn't the problem, but the father was.

"How could getting anywhere near Russ be a good thing?"

"Russ shook me out of my self-destructive behavior. And he helped me make a decision—no more musicians." She'd just put a nail in the coffin of any off chance they could possibly have anything more than friendship. But it was for the best. Brant deserved better and she certainly couldn't saddle him with Russ's baby if she figured out a way to keep the baby.

Brant cleared his throat and stood. "You know, not all musicians are bad news."

"No. But I'm done. With men in general—but especially with musicians. And besides I've got a baby to concentrate on." She trailed her fingers across the ivories again, this time with enough pressure to elicit soft tones. "If we're going to practice, we better get to it."

"Uh, yeah." Brant flipped through the songbook. "How about 'Amazing Grace'?"

Was it her imagination? Or did he seem disappointed that she'd sworn off musicians?

Mid-June tipped the nineties and despite the air-conditioning, the courtroom seemed stuffy from compressed body heat.

Yesterday Brant had sat with Tori, Jenna and Garrett during jury selection. Brant could have saved the state a lot of time and a lot of money.

Twelve people called at a time. Half a dozen questions posed by the lawyers before anyone asked if any of the twelve had a good reason they couldn't serve. Everything from running a one-man business to caretaker for an elderly family member excused half the twelve. Six more were called and the process started over.

Why not ask the entire jury pool if they had good reason they were unable to serve? Get those out of the way and then begin with the real questions on who was left instead of twelve at a time. Sheesh, at the rate jury selection had gone, he'd been amazed they'd had a jury by the end of the day.

Today Russ's trial had begun. Brant's glare settled on Russ. Russ's jaw clenched, but his gaze darted away.

Coward.

And now Brant had to sit here in court and look at Russ for the second day in a row. The man who'd beaten Tori up. The man whose baby grew inside her. The man who had no right to be a father or even live for that matter. Unfortunately Brant couldn't jump him.

If he'd known that day in the store what he knew now, he'd have pummeled Russ into mincemeat until the police arrived. But if he had, he wouldn't be able to sit here and support Tori now.

She looked shaky after her emotional testimony. Tiny compared to the mass of Russ. The big bully—it took a tiny man to raise a fist to a woman. Especially a pregnant woman.

But she'd told her story in blow-by-blow style as much as Russ's lawyer would allow and Brant had vicariously lived each of the beatings during her testimony. Brant felt like settling things himself. It was a wonder the baby had survived that last beating.

The baby was still undetectable to anyone who didn't know. Even at four months. But Brant had noticed the small bump where her stomach used to be flat. She'd taken precautions today with a loose blouse and short sleeved blazer.

Garrett, Tori and the other cowboys had testified. And now it was Brant's turn.

"Mr. McConnell, please tell the court when you first met Tori Eaton?" The prosecutor managed a casual stance.

"February fifteenth."

"Please explain the circumstances of that meeting."

"My friend, Garrett Steele, had offered to let me stay at his guesthouse any time I wanted, so I wouldn't have to commute from my Fort Worth apartment to Aubrey to serve as the song director for our church." A bead of sweat trickled between his shoulder blades. "On that night, I'd performed at the Fort Worth Championship Rodeo and decided to drive on to Aubrey and stay in Garrett's guesthouse."

"And did you stay in the guesthouse as planned?"

"No. When I got there, Tori Eaton was staying there."

"Why did your friend offer you the guesthouse if it was already occupied?"

"Tori's arrival was a bit of an emergency. Russ Dawson had beaten her up and…"

"Objection, Your Honor." Russ's court-appointed lawyer sprang to his feet. "Leading the witness to supposition."

Sweat stopped trickling and started rolling down Brant's spine. Couldn't somebody bump the thermostat down?

The prosecutor held up his hand. "I'll withdraw the line of questioning. Was there anything interesting about your encounter with Ms. Eaton?"

"She had a black eye and she threatened me with a fire poker."

"Why do you think she threatened you with a fire poker?"

"She was frightened. She didn't know I was coming and she'd just been beaten up by…"

"Objection, Your Honor." Russ's lawyer jumped up again. "Supposition."

"Overruled." The judge turned to Brant. "Please, no elaboration, Mr. McConnell. Just answer the questions."

Brant clamped his mouth shut. *I'm trying. But you won't let me.*

"When did you next see Ms. Eaton, Mr. McConnell?" The prosecutor shot him a we-went-over-this look.

"On February twentieth."

"And where did you see her?"

"I was shopping in a gift store at the Fort Worth Stockyards. The manager of the shop told us there was trouble next door at Worthwhile Designs and the owner needed our help. I ran over there with several other men."

"And what did you see when you arrived at Worthwhile Designs?" The attorney's polished shoes clicked across the hardwood flooring.

"I saw Tori Eaton cornered by Russ Dawson."

"Objection, Your Honor."

"Your Honor." The prosecutor turned to the judge. "If I may, I'd like to learn why Mr. McConnell felt Ms. Eaton was cornered."

"Objection denied." The judge finally ruled in their favor.

Russ's lawyer did a cinematic sigh and sank into his chair.

The snake-bellied lawyer hadn't given any of the other cowboys this much trouble. Maybe he'd saved all his venom for Brant because he was the final witness? Or come to think of it, the other cowboys hadn't colored their testimony with opinion. Because they hadn't gotten to know Tori. Or fallen in love with her.

"Mr. McConnell. Why did you get the impression that Mr. Dawson had Ms. Eaton cornered?"

"She was in a corner of the store facing him. He was facing her, standing close to her with a piece of jagged glass in his hand."

"How close?" The attorney approached a bailiff. "Pretend Mr. Proctor is Ms. Eaton. Tell me when to stop."

Brant waited until the prosecutor stood a foot away from the bailiff. "There."

"Did he say anything to her after you arrived?"

"No."

"What did he do?" The attorney turned back to face Brant.

"He tried to get away. But we managed to block him off."

"And what did he do after the police arrived?"

"He tried to get away again and threw a punch. But they managed to cuff him."

No objection. Maybe because the punch was in the police report.

"Your witness." The prosecutor turned to Russ's attorney.

Russ's lawyer stood—cocky and sure of himself. Defending a man who'd beaten a woman up. How did the man sleep at night?

"Mr. McConnell. Who else was in the store when you arrived?"

"Jenna Steele, the owner, was there."

"And what was Mrs. Steele doing?"

"She was—" Brant bit his lip to keep from smiling "—holding a bronze statue over her head like a weapon."

"Is it possible that Mr. Dawson was the one cornered?"

"No. Mrs. Steele was nowhere near him. She was simply—"

"Is it possible my client was merely helping to pick up the glass in an effort to help clean up the mess he'd accidentally made when he accidentally knocked the lamps over?"

Really? Brant considered his words before answering. "I can see accidentally breaking one lamp, but six?"

"Mr. McConnell. Answer the question. Yes or no."

"Well if he was trying to help clean up, he wasn't doing a very good job of it. He only picked up one measly piece of glass."

"Mr. McConnell," the judge barked. "If you continue to color your testimony with your opinion, I'll be forced to hold you in contempt. Answer the question—yes or no."

Brant's mouth went dry and his mind went blank. "To be honest, Your Honor, I've forgotten what the question was."

The judge's mouth flatlined.

"Scout's honor."

"Mr. McConnell." The lawyers's tone let on that he was as fed up as the judge was. "Is it possible my client was merely helping to pick up the glass in an effort to help clean up the mess he'd accidentally made when he accidentally knocked the lamps over?"

The judge's face was set in stone. Just waiting for Brant to mess up again. Brant caught Tori's gaze and wished he could tell her how sorry he was for what he was about to say.

Chapter 8

"Yes." Surely Brant's ears would billow steam.

Tori gave him a weak smile.

"And the punch you mentioned earlier. Did my client punch anyone?"

"No." He tried to punch a Texas Ranger but he was too drunk to land it. But if Brant mentioned that, he might end up as Russ's cell mate and unable to help Tori.

"No further questions." The rotten lawyer with no conscience turned away and reclaimed his seat beside Russ.

"You're excused, Mr. McConnell." Brant stood and returned to his seat with Garrett and Jenna.

"Fifteen-minute recess." The judge banged his gavel.

"All rise."

Everyone stood as the judge left the courtroom.

"For a minute there I thought you were gonna be keeping Dawson company in jail," Garrett whispered.

"That no-account lawyer of his wouldn't let me say half of what I had to say and twisted what I did say." His gaze caught Tori's. "I'm sorry."

"It's not your fault." She closed her eyes.

"Don't worry." Jenna patted Tori's arm. "We've still got the trump card. Everything Russ Dawson did in my store was caught on tape."

* * *

The jury wouldn't look at Tori. Was that a good sign or a bad sign? She scanned their expressions, but couldn't read them.

All eyes had been glued to the large screen in the middle of the courtroom as the surveillance tape from the store played. How could Russ think the tape would show anything in his favor?

Tori had shivered as she watched Russ purposely knock over the lamps, then stoop long enough to pick up the glass, and advance toward her another step.

But without hearing what he'd said to her, with a huge stretch of imagination, could it look like he picked up the glass to help clean up? She'd told the courtroom what he'd said to her—his veiled threat—before he broke the lamps, but that was early this morning. Would the jury even remember her testimony? Surely, there was no way anyone could think he'd broken the lamps by accident.

Now they waited for the jury's decision. *Lord, please let them see the truth.*

"Has the jury reached a verdict?"

"We have, Your Honor," the jury foreman answered.

He looked like a nice man—not the kind who would threaten or hit a woman—as he handed the bailiff a piece of paper.

The judge took the paper and read it. His gaze met Tori's then flicked to Russ. "On the charge of damage to property, this court finds the defendant guilty."

Tori gasped.

"On the charge of drunk and disorderly conduct, this court finds the defendant guilty. On the charge of terroristic threats, this court finds the defendant guilty."

The pressure slipped from her chest and she breathed fully for the first time in months.

"This court will reconvene in a week for the sentencing phase. Until then, Mr. Dawson will remain in custody. Court adjourned." The judge rapped his gavel.

"All rise."

As everyone stood, her gaze caught Russ's. Pure evil and hate emanated from him.

Oh, God, when he gets out, what will he do to me?

The pressure settled across her chest again and she trembled as a deputy led him away.

Brant's arms came around her and her shaking grew worse.

"It's okay. He can't hurt you anymore," he whispered.

But his tender words couldn't stop her trembling. The tears came and once again she soaked his shoulder.

"It's over." Jenna rubbed comforting strokes on Tori's back and pressed a tissue into her hand.

It. Would. Never. Be. Over.

"No." Tori peeled herself off Brant and mopped her face. "He'll get out. Probably sooner rather than later."

"We've got a restraining order against him and you can stay at the ranch as long as you need to."

But even if she stayed at the ranch, she wasn't there 24/7. And men like Russ didn't obey restraining orders.

"I can't stay there forever. I'm twenty-eight years old. At some point, I need to get a place of my own."

"We'll worry about all of that later." Jenna turned to Mitch. "How long do you think he'll get?"

"Well the domestic abuse charges didn't stick and neither did the resisting arrest. My math comes out to $4500 in fines or 360 days in jail."

"That's less than a year," Tori wailed.

"Yes, but he couldn't make bail. So he probably won't be able to pay the fine." Mitch checked his watch. "I gotta get back to the office."

"Thanks for your help." Jenna took up the social graces Tori had forgotten all about.

"Yes. Thank you."

Her friends flanked her, leading her out of the courthouse.

"Wanna ride with me?" Brant shot her a wink. "We could swing through McDonald's."

A bubble of laughter caught in her throat and turned into a sob.

Back in Brant's arms with Jenna rubbing her back—both murmuring soothing words.

But despite her fear and defeat, his arms sure felt good around her.

Powerless. Brant had never felt so powerless.

Mitch had been right. Russ got $4500 in fines or 360 days. He couldn't come up with the money, so he was in prison. But what if he managed to scrape up the fine?

How would Brant keep Tori and her baby safe?

All he could do was stay near. So here he was. At Jenna's store.

The bell dinged above the door as June's hot breath shoved him inside. Tori was helping a customer amongst the artwork and bronze statues.

"Hey, Brant, nice seeing you here again." Jenna wore a knowing smile.

"I thought I might buy something for the house."

"You don't like my decor?" Jenna propped her hands on her hips.

"I didn't say that." Brant laughed. "Let's just say it's a bit satiny and lacy for my nephew and me. We need something to man it up."

"Hmph. Typically male. What did you have in mind?"

His gaze strayed to Tori.

"I see. You just look around and let me know if you need any help."

"Thanks."

Jenna busied herself with some sort of catalog at the counter, leaving Brant free to watch Tori in peace. The customer was indecisive, but Tori's smile never slipped as she made suggestions and showed the lady items.

Come on, lady, buy something and move it along.

Tori noticed him. "Jenna, Mrs. McLemore is interested in your custom designs."

"Great." Jenna left her catalog. "I'll show you what we can do."

Thankfully, Jenna took over and Tori slipped away.

"Hey."

"Hey." He felt like he was in high school again. Tongue-tied over a girl.

"I got the impression you were waiting for me."

"I was looking for something to make the new house more manly." He cleared his throat. "Hunter and I are tired of lace. We need to make it our house instead of Jenna's. And I was wondering if you'd like to come to the rodeo this weekend and see my show?"

"Um, I'm not really rodeo material."

"Oh." A knot lodged in his throat. "Well, it's just that while Garrett was the headliner, people came to the rodeo in droves. Since he left and I stepped in, attendance has fallen off." He infused *poor me* into his tone and hunched his shoulders pitifully. "I'm trying to drum up the crowd, so I don't lose my job."

And got a grin out of her. "And you think me coming—just one person—will help."

"Every seat occupied counts. And you could tell two friends. And they could tell two friends. And..."

"Okay, I'll come. And I'll even tell some friends."

"I knew you wouldn't let me down."

But his knees might.

Tori had barely said two words since Brant had picked her up.

They made beautiful music together for the Lord. But she made it clear she wanted nothing more. Could he live with that and not want more?

Brant pulled his truck into the Stockyards main drag. Cars inched along the narrow brick street and the sidewalks teemed with pedestrians.

Since Tori didn't work weekends, he'd purposely chosen Saturday night. That way she couldn't walk across the street to the rodeo after work. Instead, he'd picked her up at the guesthouse. Like a date.

This was the first time he'd been alone with her since the guitar lesson. Since their musician discussion. And they hadn't shared that kind of openness or closeness since. She'd definitely kept him at arm's length except that day in the courtroom when she'd been upset.

"Where do you want to eat?"

"Eat?"

"You know, you scoop up food with your fork and shove it in your mouth. Only women usually do it more daintily than that."

"Smart aleck." Her smile softened her words. "I thought we were going to the rodeo."

"We are, but I need some supper. How 'bout you? You're eating for two."

"We ate already."

"Oh." That's what he got for trying to turn her agreeing to go to the rodeo into a date. A growling stomach.

"You can eat if you want though. I'll stop in the store or check out the gift shop."

Not exactly what he'd had in mind. "No biggie, I'll grab something at the concession stand."

"I don't want to ruin your supper."

"You dissing the concession stand?"

"No. But you obviously had something more in mind."

A lot more. "It's fine. I love their pulled pork sandwiches anyway."

He parked in the back and before he could get around and open her door, she was out of the truck.

But midstride, she stopped and clutched her stomach. Something was wrong. "You okay?"

"I think the baby's moving."

"Really?" He grinned.

But she didn't. Her eyes got too shiny. Like she was gonna burst into tears.

"It's a good thing for the baby to move right? Lets ya know everything's okay."

"Yeah. It just surprised me." She blinked several times, sniffed, and started walking again. "So, you use the back entrance?"

"It's for staff. I'll get you to your seat, then worry about my own belly." He ushered her to the entrance and through the back lobby.

"Whew! It's rank in here." She pinched her nose.

He hadn't even thought about the manure. "It won't make you sick, will it?"

"No." Her voice sounded nasally with her nose closed off. "I just wasn't expecting it. Only good-smelling food makes me sick. Manure takes getting used to."

"Have you never been to the rodeo?"

"No."

"Well, I'm honored to expose you. Are you gonna walk around like that all night?"

She removed her fingers from her nose, but held her breath. Squeezing her eyes closed, she inhaled.

"You get used to it. I don't even smell it anymore."

"Or it burns all your sinus passages out, so you can't smell anything anymore."

They rounded the arena, past the bull chutes where he saw a gathering of familiar women. "Jenna and Garrett probably won't be here. He thinks he'll sidetrack people away from me, but he does that without even being here."

"It's not you. He's just…"

"GARRETT STEELE. Trust me, I know."

"Maybe if you'd stayed in Nashville longer than a year, you'd be BRANT MCCONNELL."

"You think?"

"Well, you're a great singer. And you're um…not hard to look at."

"Really?"

A pretty blush tinted her cheeks.

"Sometimes, I'm glad I didn't catch my break in Nashville." Like now.

"Why?"

"I look at Garrett. He has to sneak around everywhere and be smuggled in and out. He can't go wherever he pleases. And the press is always after him." He was just gonna say it. "And I might never have met you."

She rolled her eyes. "No big loss there."

"You're wrong, Tori."

"Brant, here's the star of our show." Natalie, publicist extraordinaire, linked her arm through Brant's. "We're expecting a big crowd tonight. I can feel it."

"I hope so. You know Tori. Don't you?"

"Sure. Hey, Tori. I've been hearing good things about you from Jenna."

"It's about time, I guess."

"This is my friend, Kendra." She gestured to a brunette. "Her husband, Stetson, is the bullfighter you'll see in action with my pickup man, Lane."

Bullfighter—it always made Brant think of a matador instead of what they called rodeo clowns these days.

"Remind me of what a pickup man is." Tori shifted in the metal chair, her shoulder brushed his, sending his heart into overdrive.

"They do for the bronc riders what the bullfighters do for the bull riders. Those cool guys who swoop in on horseback and rescue the cowboy from the bronc's back after the buzzer or if the rider gets in trouble." Natalie gestured to a blond. "And this is Lacie. Her husband, Quinn, is announcing tonight. Caitlyn's still queen for a little longer, so she won't be able to sit with us."

"Caitlyn's quitting?"

"She gave her notice." Natalie bit her lip. "She's pregnant."

Something passed over Tori's expression, but it was gone so quick, Natalie didn't seem to notice.

She caught Brant's glance. "Don't you need to go get your food?"

"I've got time. I'd just as soon sit here with all these good-looking ladies for a bit."

"Married ladies." Kendra laughed.

"Being married makes you off-limits, but it doesn't mean you quit being good-looking."

"I like this guy." Kendra winked at Tori. "You should go for him, Tori."

"You could join our rodeo family." Natalie elbowed her.

Tori's face went from pink to crimson.

Even other people could see how perfect they were for each other.

But Tori wasn't interested. She was determined to avoid musicians and be a single mom.

It was probably a good thing that their relationship would never develop into more. No, he wouldn't be like her dad or the other musicians she'd known. But if he got his big break, he wouldn't be hanging his hat in Aubrey for long anyway.

So, why couldn't he leave her alone?

The spotlight shone on Brant in the center of the arena and his gravelly voice tugged at Tori. The love song's pure, sweet words sung by him ought to bring women to the rodeo in droves.

Why did he have to be so devastatingly handsome, so charming, so gentle? Why did he have to be a musician? Why did her world have to be so complicated?

The baby fluttered in her stomach again, like moth wings inside her. How could she contemplate giving her baby away as she felt the movement? But she had to keep the baby safe.

As his second song ended, Natalie stood and headed toward the back lobby. Minutes later, Brant strode toward them from the bull chutes and reclaimed his seat beside Tori. Great. She'd been more comfortable with him gone.

He leaned close and cupped his hands around Tori's ear. "I know you don't know Nat very well, but could you go make sure she's okay? She was crying. Bull riding is starting and I know Kendra doesn't like to miss Stetson in action."

"Sure." Great, she knew Nat through Jenna. They'd never had a conversation that didn't include Jenna. They'd never been in the same room without Jenna.

How could she help?

Natalie probably wouldn't even talk to her.

"Where did she go?" Tori asked.

"To Caitlyn's dressing room. I'll show you." Brant stood and she followed.

Past the bull chutes, to the back lobby and a row of doors.

"That one." Brant pointed. "I'll leave y'all alone, but let

me know if she needs anything. I can get Lane, get her a ride home—whatever she needs."

Tori cleared her throat and knocked on the dressing room door. "Natalie, it's Tori. Brant wanted me to check on you. Are you all right?"

The door opened. Natalie grabbed her arm and pulled her inside, then shut the door. "Great, the whole place knows I'm bawling."

"Brant's worried about you, but I'm the only one he told. I know we don't know each other that well, but I'd like to help if I can. And Brant said to let him know if you need anything. Should he get Lane or do you need a ride home maybe?"

"How about a baby?" Natalie paced the room. "Can you give me a baby?"

Chapter 9

Tori's heart stilled in her chest. "A baby? I don't understand."

Natalie's heels clicked across the floor—back and forth. "Back before I was a Christian, I slept around all over the place. And the one time I forgot to use protection, I got pregnant with Hannah. I wasn't ready to be a mom then and I gave her to her father."

Natalie sank into a chair. "But I'm different now. I've done everything I know to do to make it up to Hannah. We have a great relationship now. And Lane is a wonderful Christian husband. We've been trying to have a baby for months. Much longer than Caitlyn and Mitch have even been married. But she's pregnant and I'm not."

"And you have to be happy for her."

"She's my sister and I love her. I am happy for her." Natalie's voice broke. "Just not for me."

Unsure of what to do, Tori put a hand on her shoulder. "Sometimes these things take time." It sounded lame even to her own ears.

"It didn't with Hannah." Natalie blew out a big sigh.

"I don't mean to be insensitive." Tori swallowed hard. "But have you thought about adopting?"

"That's what Lane said. He says we're in no rush, but if nothing happens after a few years, we can adopt."

But Tori didn't have a few years. She needed a mother

for her baby in about four-and-a-half months. "There are lots of babies who need good homes."

"Adoption kind of scares me." Natalie shook her head. "Kendra and Stetson adopted their daughter. And her biological family has come out of the woodwork ever since. Kendra spent months worrying someone would file for custody."

"And?"

"No one did."

"Does Kendra regret adopting?"

"No."

"It's complicated, but it turned out okay."

"Yes." Natalie shrugged. "But on top of that, Hannah isn't Lane's. I wish she was—but she's not. You'd never know it from the way he loves her, but I'd like to reward him for loving us both so much by giving him his own child."

"I can understand that. But it's obvious he can love someone else's child, so I just thought..."

"Thanks for checking on me." Natalie swiped underneath her eyes with her thumbs and checked the mirror. "Sorry for dumping everything on you, but I can't really share this with Caitlyn or Jenna. I can't let them know Caitlyn's pregnancy upset me. I won't take an iota of their happiness away by making them worry about me."

"Not a word from me."

"Thanks." Natalie stood. "By the way, I wish my statement had helped your case."

Tori's brain spun. "What statement?"

"Back when I was in my barhopping mode, this guy got a little rough with me. Mitch was on a stakeout and rescued me, so when Mitch made that arrest at Jenna's store, he recognized him."

Tori shuddered.

"Mitch asked me to file a report to show a pattern of violence. But the judge ruled it inadmissible."

"Thanks for trying."

"Now, I need to get myself together—pull myself out of this pity party and go watch my husband save some cowboys. Tell Brant I'm fine and I'll be out in a bit."

"Sure." Tori hurried out of the dressing room. So she wasn't the first woman Russ had gotten rough with. She wouldn't be the last. And her baby would never be safe.

She had four-and-a-half months to convince Natalie she had the perfect solution. For both of them.

The lunch lull had hit the store. Crazy busy for a Monday. Tori straightened items on shelves and whisked the feather duster over the lamps and sculptures. Brant's gravelly voice played through her mind—singing a Country song she couldn't get out of her head. Along with Natalie's tear-streaked cheeks.

"How was the rodeo?" Jenna's question shook Tori from her reverie.

"Good. Very exciting actually."

"The Brant part? Or the rodeo event part?"

Actually, the Natalie part. "Brant has a great voice and it was weird hearing him sing Country love songs when I'm used to him singing hymns. But I actually meant the bronc and bull riding. I never knew how exciting those events were." Tori shrugged. "It was kind of fun."

"I love Brant's voice. While Garrett's is the perfect smooth baritone, Brant has that rough quality and it comes out more when he sings country music."

Tori rolled her eyes and made a great show of carefully dusting a lamp with a leather shade and stitching. "I'm not interested in Brant."

"Why? He's such a great guy. And you could use a great guy about now."

"After Russ, I swore off musicians and besides, I'm pregnant, Jenna. With Russ's baby."

"I didn't know Russ was a musician."

"Not a very good one." If she spent any more time on the lamp, Jenna would be onto her. She turned to the bronze statues she'd already dusted. "The play-guitar-in-a-bar-with-no-future-prospects kind."

"Oh. Well, I have it on good authority that Brant is the kind of musician who'd raise another man's child as his own."

"He's nice. But I don't know if he's that nice. And even if I were interested, asking him or any other man to take on Russ's child wouldn't be fair to them."

"You should let Brant make that call." Jenna rearranged a display of seashells and driftwood candleholders from her new beachy collection.

"We're friends—that's all. And I told him I've sworn off musicians."

"Why would you tell him that?"

"Because I don't want him getting any ideas."

"Then why did you go to the rodeo with him?"

Tori sighed. "Because he gave me some song and dance about how attendance has been down since Garrett left."

"It's true. And I feel bad for him. Garrett's a tough act to follow."

"I imagine he knew that going in." Subject change in order. "So when do you and Garrett leave for his tour?"

"Actually." Jenna shrugged. "Garrett left after Russ's trial."

Tori shot her the look. "Weren't you supposed to go with him?"

"With Russ…and everything else going on, I didn't feel like it was a good time for me to leave."

"Oh, Jenna." Tori squeezed her eyes shut. "I can't believe you stayed here to babysit me."

"It's fine. Garrett will only be gone two months. I'll fly out and visit a couple of times. And it's not only you I feel the need to babysit. Caitlyn just found out she's pregnant."

The perfect opportunity to broach the subject. "Yeah, Natalie told me at the rodeo."

"Did she seem okay about it?" Jenna plopped on the stool by the register.

"She seemed fine." Tori crossed her fingers behind her back. Were Christians supposed to tell little white lies? "She did tell me she and Lane have been trying to get pregnant, but nothing's happened."

"Really. I'm surprised she shared that. I told her it hasn't been that long—to relax and be patient."

"Do you think she and Lane would adopt my baby?"

Jenna's jaw dropped. "You're thinking about giving your baby up?"

"I can't—" Tori blew out a big breath "—keep the baby. Not with Russ lurking around."

"Russ is in prison."

"True, but you're uneasy enough about how long he'll stay there, that you ditched touring with Garrett." Tori hugged herself. "I'll never be free of Russ once he finds out about the baby. And I can't subject any child to that."

"Maybe he'll be the kind of man who walks away."

"No. Russ is all about control. The baby gives him control." The baby moved and Tori pressed a hand to her side. "The baby's moving."

Jenna's gaze met hers. "Can I feel?"

"Sure." Tori guided Jenna's hand to the movement.

"I felt Caitlyn's baby yesterday." Jenna rubbed her hand in a circular motion and the fluttering inside Tori increased. "No movement yet, but I always thought a pregnant belly would be all soft and squishy like fat. But it's hard as a rock."

A huge knot cut off anything Tori could think of to say. Her vision blurred.

"So you've given this a lot of thought? It's a big decision. Not something you go into lightly."

"I've prayed about it." Tori bit her quivering lip. "The only way to keep the baby safe is to give him or her up."

"And you think you can do that?"

"If I find the right parents, I'll know it's for the best."

"If I get Nat on board." Jenna pulled her hand away. "You cannot change your mind."

"I know. Nat told me about Kendra's drama."

Jenna's eyes squeezed shut. "You talked to Nat about adopting your baby?"

"No. I brought up adoption, but I didn't tell her I'm pregnant."

"Can I tell her you're pregnant?"

"It's getting pretty obvious. She may suspect. But tell her to keep it quiet."

"Or course." Jenna sucked in a deep breath. "Let me handle this. It's a touchy subject, but I'll feel her out."

"Thanks." Tori pressed her hand to the slight bump where her stomach used to be flat. As slender and lean as she was, clothing wouldn't camouflage much longer.

Could she give her baby up? Her thoughts went to Russ. His anger, his possessiveness, his brutality. She shivered. There was no could to it.

She had to. She had to give her baby up. She had to stop thinking of the baby as hers.

The baby. For whatever reason, God had entrusted her with this child. She had to do right by the baby.

Tired to the bone and all she'd done was play piano at church this morning. The congregation had unanimously voted her in as pianist at the close of the service. The show of acceptance and love had relaxed her taught nerves.

But simply accepting all the hugs and handshakes as she stood in the church lobby with Brother Thomas and Brant exhausted her.

The doctor had warned Tori she'd be excessively tired and he obviously knew what he was talking about. How could the tiny bean-shaped spot she'd seen on the ultrasound screen make her so tired?

But the baby wasn't tiny anymore. The doctor had insisted on an ultrasound this month because of the beating and her stress level, but she'd refused to look at the screen. Seeing it would make her want to keep the baby.

The baby. Not her baby. She'd do whatever she had to to protect the baby.

"You're doing great, Tori." The pastor patted her shoulder.

"Thanks."

"You have a gift." Brant caught her gaze and try as she might she couldn't pull herself away from those jade eyes. "The best pianists follow the director and cover his flubs. You're a natural."

"Thanks." Move feet. "But I didn't hear any flubs."

"Cuz you covered 'em for me." He shot her a knee-dissolving grin. "Hey, my sister and nephew are meeting me for lunch at Moms on Main. Care to join us?"

"Um. That sounds nice, but I think I'll go home. I'm tired—maybe a nap between services."

"You look tired."

"Thanks a lot."

"No, I mean, you look great. Just tired."

Her feet finally took the hint and she slipped out the exit. But halfway across the parking lot, footfalls advanced on her and she turned to see Brant following. Her heart did a little flutter and the baby did, too.

"Hey." He kicked at the gravel with the toe of his boot. "I forgot to invite you to our Fourth of July picnic."

"Picnic?"

"At the house. Raquel's cooking up a feast. Our folks are coming to see the new place."

"Your parents are coming?"

"They weren't overly excited when we moved away from Pleasant Valley and always hoped we'd move home someday. Our buying the house in Aubrey was hard on them—the end of their dream. Raquel invited them for dinner so that they can see we're settled and happy here."

"I don't know." She closed her eyes. "Meeting your family?"

"Part of our being happy here is making friends. I'd like my new friends to meet my family. Jenna's coming, too."

How stupid of her. Why else would he want her to meet his family? "Oh. Well…"

"And you'd be doing me a favor. Raquel has a tendency to focus on Hunter to the exclusion of everyone else. I'd like her to make some friends. Come on, she's a great cook and she loves having people to cook for. The baby will love it."

She couldn't hide her smile. "Okay. It sounds nice."

Nerves prickling and a trail of sweat trickling down her spine, Tori trailed behind Jenna up the steps of the ranch-style house where Jenna lived before she married Garrett.

"This is weird." Jenna rang her former doorbell.

The last time Tori had been here, a year and a half ago, she'd been dog drunk. Now, Brant and his sister had bought the house and here she was crashing his family's Fourth of July picnic, meeting Brant's sister. And his parents.

What had she been thinking? Brant had said he wanted his family to meet his friends.

Friends? Jenna fit the category, but Tori wanted to be much more than friends. Since that could never be, she should keep her distance from him. But she couldn't seem to stay away.

He beckoned and she came running—like a lovesick puppy. A pregnant-with-someone-else's-child lovesick puppy. Oh why couldn't she have met Brant before she met Russ?

If only she'd driven her own car, she could slink away. Tell Brant later that she hadn't been feeling well. True. Her insides roiled.

The door swung open and Brant stood there grinning at her.

Her roiling insides melted into a puddle with one glimpse of him.

"Come on in. Meet the folks." Brant gestured to the lineup waiting in the entryway. "Mom, Dad, Raquel and Hunter." He tousled the little boy's hair.

She could see Brant in both of his parents. His mom had dark hair and his green eyes, while Raquel's blond hair and blue eyes came from their dad. Hunter had dark hair and brown eyes he must have gotten from his father.

"This is Garrett's wife, Jenna Steele, and Tori Eaton, our church pianist."

Much ado was made over Garrett with Brant's family going on about how much they loved his music since he'd switched to Christian Country.

"I'm sorry." Brant's mom approached and took Tori's hand in both of hers. "It's just that Brant has told us so much about Garrett. We're so glad to meet Brant's friends."

But nothing about his pregnant piano player friend. "Nice to meet you, too."

His mom linked arms with Tori. "Supper's almost ready."

As they made their way to the kitchen, Tori noticed the decor. Jenna's satin drapery was gone. In it's place— cowboy. Cowhide curtain toppers, tan suede furnishings and turquoise throw pillows with conchos and fringe. Not a hint of lace in sight.

Come to think of it, Brant hadn't bought anything in the store that day to *man up* Jenna's house. Had he only come to the store to invite her to the rodeo?

His mom ushered her into the kitchen.

Nerves prickled and she fought the urge to smooth a hand over her stomach. In just over a week, she'd be five months along. Her white blouse wasn't maternity, but it was loose and flowing with crotched sleeves to hopefully draw the eye up. With nondescript denim capris and cute red wedge sandals, maybe she could pull off a summery, casual look. Hopefully, a not-pregnant look.

Grease and bird assaulted her senses.

Fried chicken.

Tori's stomach turned. "Bathroom?"

Brant must have seen it in her face. He grabbed her arm and propelled her down a hallway.

She didn't have the strength to protest as he ushered her in the bathroom and shut the door behind them.

Once again, he held her hair until she finished. She flushed and closed the lid, then sank onto it.

"You know you didn't have to come with me."

"I had to make sure you were okay."

"No one ever died because of morning sickness."

"It's not morning." Brant grinned.

"Sometimes a smell triggers it no matter what time of day it is. Or night."

"Will you be okay now?"

"Usually, once it's done I'm good. What must your family think?"

"I guess I'll have to tell them what's going on."

Her eyes grew huge. "No. I'm leaving. You can tell them I'm coming down with something."

"Not a good idea. Raquel's been attending their old

church in Garland to transition Hunter, but she's planning to end up at our church eventually." He knelt beside her and handed her a washcloth. "She'll probably join and she's the type of member who shows up. She'll eventually realize you're pregnant. Especially if y'all become friends. And if we try to hide your pregnancy now, they'll think the baby's mine."

"We don't want that. I guess you're right." She covered her face with the washcloth, cool against her heated skin. "They'll think I'm such a slut."

"I don't want to hear that word from you again." He pulled her hands away and gently gripped her chin until she looked at him. "That's not who you are. My family is Christian. If you'll let them, they'll love you."

"I'm so embarrassed. I barely meet them and scurry off to throw up with their son in tow."

"Nothing to be embarrassed about. You're a lovely woman doing the right thing by your baby." He stood, opened a drawer under the sink and pulled out a new toothbrush still in the package. "Raquel always keeps spares."

"Is that a kind way of saying my breath stinks?"

"No. That's a kind way of helping you feel better."

"I feel like I need a shower."

"It's all yours."

"I can't take a shower. Your family will think I'm pregnant and nuts."

"You look fine. Just freshen up a bit and I'll go explain things." He started for the door.

She closed her eyes. "I should go with you."

"No need." He stopped and turned to face her again. "Tori, please don't leave."

"I won't." She couldn't let them think he was responsible for the mess she'd made.

"Take your time." Brant stepped out of the bathroom.

What kind of man held a woman's hair while she threw up? Not once, but twice.

The kind of man she'd given up on ever meeting. If only she'd done things right. If only she could've met Brant and married him before she'd trashed her life. If only this baby was his and they could raise their child together.

But it was too late for that. Snap out of the fantasy.

She turned the water on and washed her face wishing she could wash away her mistakes as easily.

Chapter 10

When Brant came out of the bathroom, his family had moved outside where Raquel had outdone herself on the Fourth of July decor.

His parents sat on the red bench on one side of the table with Jenna across from them on the long barnwood bench. Red, white and blue plates, cups and settings flanked the red-and-white-striped tablecloth, with heavy-headed sunflowers in a blue pitcher.

But it wouldn't be the celebration they'd planned. Not after he broke the news.

"Is Tori all right?" Raquel gave him a knowing look. She knew. Must be women's intuition. Did Mom know, too?

No. His mom looked worried.

"Where's Hunter?"

"In the loft." Raquel pointed to the barn. "Out of earshot."

"I'll go check on Tori." Jenna stood and headed toward the house.

Brant didn't know how to tell them, other than to just say it. "Tori's pregnant."

Mom gasped.

"Son?" His father's one word summed up the unspoken question.

"It's not my baby."

A single sigh whooshed from both of his parents.

"Of course not." Mom shook her head.

"We shouldn't have even thought it." Dad put an arm around Mom's shoulders. "Sorry, son, we were…"

"Shocked. It's okay. Tori hasn't been a Christian long. Before she became a Christian, she was involved with an abusive boyfriend."

"And it's his child?" Raquel poured herself another glass of tea.

"Yes."

"This sounds dangerous." Mom pressed a hand to her heart.

"I can handle this guy—if and when he gets out of prison."

"Why is he in prison?" Dad asked.

"Long story. Listen, Tori will be out in a minute. She needs your support. I need your support. We need your support."

"You're involved with her?" Mom's gaze never left his.

"We're friends."

"Son." Caution filled Dad's tone. "You know we love you and we'll support you, but you must know this smacks of Tiffany."

"It's not like that." Brant growled.

The back screen door slammed shut. Brant looked up.

Jenna and Tori emerged from the house. The woman he loved. His future.

No matter what his family said.

"Want me to take you home?" Brant wasn't ready to let Tori go yet as he walked her to Jenna's car.

"That would be silly. I can ride with Jenna."

"I guess I'll see you at church then."

"Guess so. Your family is great. Thank them for being so kind and understanding." She turned away.

Leaving him to face his family again. Alone.

Might as well get it over with. He stalked back to the house, ready for battle.

Earlier, Tori had emerged from the bathroom and rescued him from their assumptions about his past history. His family had been gracious to her—Mom and Raquel had even shared their pregnancies with Tori.

But now they were alone.

He stepped inside. Both of his parents waited to pounce in the foyer.

"Brant, how on earth did this happen again?" Dad's tone was incredulous.

"Bad luck I guess. I seem to find the perfect woman, but after it's too late."

"You're setting yourself up to be hurt." Mom joined the chorus. "Again."

At least Raquel was upstairs getting Hunter ready for bed, so he wouldn't have to appease her yet.

"I'm not, Mom. I'm being a friend. And Tori needs a friend."

"You went in the bathroom with her while she threw up, son. A man doesn't generally do such a thing unless he's in love." Dad put his arm around Mom's waist. "Trust me, I know."

"I went with her because I knew she'd be terribly embarrassed." They didn't have to know it wasn't the first time or that he'd held her hair each time. "I thought she might slip out and walk home."

"You say the father is in prison. What about when he gets out?" Worry shone clear in Mom's eyes.

Proof that they had nothing against Tori or her past bad choices. They were only concerned for their son. He had to keep a tight reign on the frustration bubbling in his chest.

"He should be there at least for a while. Tori's not telling him about the baby and she has a restraining order against him."

"Just think about this long and hard, son." Dad pursed his lips as if he were choosing his words carefully. "This whole situation reminds your mother and me of Tiffany."

"Me, too."

"We don't mean to hurt you." Mom tried this time. "But your father and I were never convinced that Tiffany loved you."

"You think I didn't know that?" he shouted.

"Shhh!" Raquel descended the stairs. "Keep it quiet down here."

"Sorry." Brant lowered his voice. "They're bringing up Tiffany."

"Well, you have to admit…" Rachel's voice trailed off.

"Okay, I'll admit it. I'm in love with Tori. But this is different. It's not like it was with Tiffany."

"You're right." Mom's tone soothed. Always the peacemaker. "You and Tiffany were young—only seventeen. Now you're twenty-eight. And Tori is…"

"Twenty-eight. I know Tiffany didn't love me. I knew it then, okay. She loved Davis and only Davis. I was the stupid one who fell in love with my best friend's girl."

"It's never stupid to fall in love." Raquel's sad gaze caught his. "It may end in an unfortunate way, but it's not stupid."

"If Tiffany's situation had been different—" Mom's gaze pierced him "—would she have turned to you?"

Brant shook his head. "Probably not. But none of that mattered to me. I loved her. And sometimes love can grow. I didn't fall for Tori the moment I saw her. It took time." Not much time, but they didn't need the details. "Maybe over time, Tori can fall for me."

"If Tori didn't have an abusive ex-boyfriend, if she wasn't pregnant, would she have turned to you?" Mom asked.

"You just admitted Tori doesn't have near the baggage

Tiffany had." Brant grinned. "And another difference—Tori hasn't turned to me. Other than church, I practically have to beg her to spend any time with me."

"But once again, you're hoping to win the love of a woman pregnant with someone else's child?" Dad sighed. "Tiffany hurt you so badly, son. It was hard for us to watch her use you."

"Tori's not like Tiffany. She's not using me." He strode past them to the living room—hoping to end the discussion. "Her family, friends and our church are supporting her. She's not turning to me because she's alone and has nowhere else to go. She's strong and she'd never…" Eleven years later, he still couldn't bring himself to say it. "She's keeping the baby."

"How does Tori feel about you?" Raquel tried to be the voice of reason.

"I don't know."

"I saw something in the way she looked at you."

His soul lit up and he caught his sister's gaze. "Really?"

"Regardless of how Tori feels about you." Mom put her hand on his arm. "I wish you could fall in love with a girl who isn't pregnant with someone else's child."

"Me, too. Trust me." The irony of the situation bubbled up inside him and came out in a tension-relieving laugh.

"We'll support you." Mom hugged him. "In whatever happens with Tori. And we'll pray for you."

"Thanks, Mom."

Was there really something about the way Tori looked at him? Hope sparked inside him. And all of his parents' well-meaning caution couldn't tamp it out.

The day had hopped with customers and threatened to suck the air-conditioning outside as a mid-July blast of hot air entered every time the door opened. Tori fielded the ready-made customers while Jenna handled the custom orders. Finally closing time. Tori pressed her hand against the small of her aching back.

With all the merchandise straightened, she shut the blinds as Jenna closed out the register.

"Your back's hurting." Jenna frowned. "You know, we can cut your hours."

"It started up this week. By the end of the day, it's killing me, but I don't want to work less." She held out her foot modeling her cute kitten heels. "I should probably stop going for style and wear my comfortable shoes."

"I have news. I talked to Nat."

Tori's insides froze. "About the baby?"

"Yes. She and Lane would like to meet with you."

"Really?" A sinking feeling settled low in Tori's stomach. As if the baby was disappointed in her. "When?"

"She wants you to call her and set something up." Jenna held a business card toward her.

Tori's hand shook as she reached for it.

"Are you sure about this?"

"I'm sure." Tori turned the card over and over between her fingers. "I'm sure this is the best thing for the baby." He or she didn't need a father like Russ lurking around. "Let's get out of here. Don't you have a hot date waiting for you in St. Louis?"

"As a matter of fact I do. Oh, how I've missed that man of mine." Jenna locked up and they walked to their cars parked side by side. "I still hate leaving you alone. Want to stay at the main house while I'm gone? Flora cooks a mean shrimp Alfredo with sun-dried tomatoes."

The mere thought of garlic turned her stomach. "I'll be fine. That whirlpool tub at the guesthouse is calling my back and you'll only be gone for the weekend."

"Mitch is on high alert if anything changes with Russ, so don't worry." Jenna put an arm around her shoulders. "I'm really proud of you, Tori. For what you're doing for your baby and the way you've turned your life around. You're like a different person—the person I always knew you could be."

A knot lodged in her throat. "Thanks."

They got in their cars and each waited to make sure their engines started, before backing out and pulling into the alley, then turning onto East Exchange—the main drag of the Fort Worth Stockyards.

Strength. *God give me strength to give this baby up.*

At the stoplight, Tori slipped her hands-free headset into place. "Call Brant."

The fancy phone did its thing and his ringtone started up—"He Set Me Free." Tori hummed along, trying to calm her nerves as the light changed and she pulled onto the highway.

"Hey." Brant's soothing voice came on the line. "You okay?"

"Not really. Can you talk?"

"Sure. I'm just watching Hunter's basketball moves. Is anything wrong?"

She hadn't even told him she was thinking about giving the baby up. Why had she called him?

"Tori?"

"I'm giving the baby up for adoption."

"You're what?" Surprise echoed in his tone.

"I'm supposed to set up a meeting with Jenna's cousin Natalie, a possible candidate." It sounded like politics instead of parenting. "I mean Jenna's cousin and her husband are possible adoptive parents."

"When did you decide this?"

"I've been thinking about it for a while." She hit her brake as a car cut in front of her.

"Let me come over. We'll talk."

"No. I'm tired and my back hurts."

"From standing on your feet all day. Raquel had that problem with Hunter."

"I just want to get in my jammies and lie down." Her vision blurred and she blinked the tears away.

"When do you plan to set up the meeting?"

"I'll have to call her and see."

"Want me to go with you?"

Her insides warmed. Without realizing it, that's why she'd called him. She needed someone in her corner. Jenna would naturally be torn, but would support her cousin. Tori needed someone to fully support her in this. And she'd known Brant would.

"Would you?"

"Or course. Just let me know when."

The baby jabbed her ribs. A protest? She patted her stomach. *I know what I'm doing, baby.* "When's the best time for you?"

"I'm free most days or any evening on Monday, Tuesday or Thursday."

"Natalie works days. Lane has his fencing company during the day and works the same rodeos you do, so we should be able work something out."

"I'll be on standby."

"I really appreciate it." Her vision blurred again.

"Not a problem. I'll help you any way I can."

"Thanks. I'll let you know as soon as I do." She wanted to keep him on the phone. Just to hear his soothing tone. But he had a life and she was out of things to say. "Talk to you soon."

How had she rated Brant as a friend? Willing to be on standby for her. A man who sensed what she needed when she didn't.

But what she wanted was him. As much more than a friend. Did he sense that?

Over the months she'd known Brant, she'd come to realize he wasn't the typical musician like she'd hung out with. But he still had an aspiration. Could she fit into his megachurch dream?

Brant hung up and the breath froze in his chest. He sank onto his tailgate.

How could Tori give up her child? Did he have her pegged wrong?

"Uncle Brant, watch this." Hunter did a clumsy spin and shot the basketball. It bounced off the rim.

"You almost made it."

The front door opened and Raquel stepped out. "Supper's ready."

"Mom, come watch."

"For a minute. We don't want the food to get cold." Raquel descended the steps and joined Brant on the tailgate. The truck barely shifted under her slight weight. She bumped his shoulder with hers. "Hey, you okay?"

"Tori's giving the baby up for adoption."

"Why?"

"I don't know. I wanted to go to her place and talk, but she said she's tired."

The fountain Raquel had bought trickled soothing water down the rock ledge. But nothing could ease his soul.

"Maybe she figures the baby would be better off with a mom and dad."

"Maybe."

"Kind of nips your fantasy of marrying her and raising her child as your own."

He turned toward her. "How did you know that?"

"Because you feel like you failed Tiffany. Tori is your chance to make up for it."

Steam would spew from his ears any minute. Brant slid off the tailgate. "You have no idea what you're talking about. I love Tori. And because her baby is a part of her, I love the baby. It has nothing to do with Tiffany."

"Okay, calm down." Raquel gestured toward Hunter. "I just want you to know, deep down in your gut, you didn't fail Tiffany. Tiffany failed Tiffany. Okay?"

"I know that. I blamed myself for a long time, but I don't anymore. I did everything I could for Tiffany."

"You did." Raquel patted his shoulder. "But she couldn't face letting her parents know she was pregnant. And she didn't love you, which I hate to speak ill of the dead, but that was pure stupidity on her part."

Her backhanded compliment simmered him down. He leaned his hip against the truck. "Tori isn't anything like Tiffany. The situation is similar, but that's all. And if Tori wasn't pregnant, I'd still love her."

"If she wasn't pregnant, everything would be easier. So support her in giving the baby up and you two could have a fresh start."

"You're right."

"So go for it."

"There's just one problem."

"What's that?"

"I don't think she really wants to give the baby up."

"Then why is she?"

"I don't know."

But he'd find out. And he'd make sure she made the right decision. For the baby. And for her.

The meeting was in an hour. Plenty of time. Brant pulled into the lot of the guesthouse and parked.

He grabbed the McDonald's bag and climbed out.

Before he ever got to the porch, Tori opened the door and his heart took a tumble and landed at her feet.

"What are you doing here? The meeting's not until seven o'clock."

"I brought comfort food and I thought we could talk. Have you eaten?"

"No. And I'm starving." She frowned. "Were you in Fort Worth today?"

"Nope."

"You drove all the way to Denton? For me?"

"It's only fifteen minutes."

Her eyes turned shimmery. "Why are you so nice to me?"

Cause I love you. "Let's see, I'm a nice guy and you haven't met up with many of those. So, I figure I need to prove to you that men can be nice and treat a lady right." He opened the bag. "Maybe if I open it out here, the smell won't hit you so hard."

"Thanks." She hugged herself—small and vulnerable. He pulled the Filet-O-Fish box out of the bag and opened it. Late July offered no breeze to waft away the slight fishy smell.

Tori stepped inside and he followed—remembering the last time he'd been here. The first night he'd met her and her fire poker. She'd brought out his protective side and his feelings for her had grown from there. If she hadn't had a black eye that night, would he have fallen for her? If she'd been happy and healthy when they'd met, would he be standing here willing his arms to stay away from her?

He'd always been tenderhearted. As a kid, he'd nursed wounded animals he found in the woods back to health. Now he nursed wounded people.

Her baby bump was more obvious at five-and-a-half months and made him go all tender inside. Who was he kidding—Tori made him go all tender inside. All by herself.

He set the food on the counter and she tore into it before he could think to bless it. He didn't want to embarrass her, so he let it go and scanned the house. Exactly as he remembered it. White stucco walls, an Austin stone fire-place, with log beams lining the ceiling. Rustic hardwood floors and leather furnishings. No personal touches, no family pictures, nothing to indicate she really lived there.

Yes it was a guesthouse, but she'd lived here for months, and Jenna wouldn't mind if she changed it up a bit. But Tori still thought of herself as a temporary guest. When he met her, she'd been battered, frightened and homeless. Now, she was pregnant, frightened and homeless.

"Did you find out if the baby is a girl or a boy yet?"

"No." Her voice wobbled a bit. "I decided I didn't want to know. It's better that way."

"Why did you decide to give the baby up?"

"Because it's for the best."

"Best for who?"

"For the baby."

"But what about for you?"

"I can't let myself think that way." She shook her head.

"Because you don't want to give the baby up?"

"I have to."

"Why, if you don't want to? You've got family and friends willing to support you. Your aunt, Jenna, Garrett, me, our church—we'll all help. You won't be in this alone, Tori."

She shook her head again. "I can't. I can't keep this baby."

"Why?" His heart ached at her obvious distress. "You'd be a great mom—just like your mom."

"Don't you see?" She set her sandwich down and tears glistened in her eyes. "I can't protect this baby. Any more than Mom could protect herself from my father."

"So, you're giving the baby up because of Russ? He's in prison."

"But not forever."

"No. But Garrett and Jenna can keep you safe. You can

stay here with the alarm system." *And someday, I'll convince you to marry me and I'll keep you safe.*

"I can't live here sponging off Garrett and Jenna forever."

"You're not sponging off them. And even if you were, I think they can afford it. You can pay rent if it bothers you."

"I've tried." Tori rolled her eyes. "Jenna won't take anything. But that's not the point. I want to stand on my own two feet and not have to worry about Russ finding out about the baby. Besides a baby needs a mother and a father. I don't have that to give."

I could help you with that. If you'd let me.

"Please, Brant." A tear spilled down her cheek. "I need you to support me on this. I can't do it by myself. And I know Aunt Loretta will try to talk me into keeping the baby. But I've thought about this and I've prayed about it.

"With everything in me, I want to keep this baby. But I have to do what's right. And sometimes—" her voice cracked "—doing what's right means giving up what you love most. I need someone I can count on in my corner. To help me through this."

Her tears fell freely now and Brant handed her a tissue. The tears were the deal breaker. He moved close to the stool where she sat and offered his shoulder.

She let out a watery laugh and laid her head against him.

"I'll be here for you." Brant's arms circled her and he wished he could hold her like this forever. "Whatever you need me to do. I'm with you, Tori."

"Thanks." She shuddered, then relaxed against him.

He'd go to the meeting with her. And he'd support her in giving the baby up. But he'd also be hoping she'd fall in love with him. And keep the baby she obviously wanted.

Chapter 11

Seated on Natalie's overstuffed plush couch in the cozy furnished, modernized farmhouse, Tori had never been so uncomfortable in her life. Brant sat beside her with Natalie and Lane across from her.

"I must say I never really thought about adoption." Natalie paused.

"I think it's too soon." Lane took Natalie's hand in his.

"So why did you ask Tori to come here?" Brant looked as if he might haul Tori over his shoulder and bolt.

"Just to talk." Natalie's voice quivered. "After Jenna told me about your pregnancy, I thought your baby might be the solution to both our problems."

"My baby isn't a problem." Tori pressed her hand to her stomach.

"I'm sorry. That was a poor choice of words." Natalie's tone soothed. "Of course your baby isn't a problem. But the baby's father is."

"Yes."

"Are you positive you want to give your child up?" Lane's stiff posture and guarded expression advertised he wasn't convinced. About any of this.

"Yes." She had no choice.

"If the baby's father weren't a threat, would you still want to adopt your child out?"

Tori closed her eyes. "I don't know."

"So you are attached to the baby?"

"Of course, she's attached to the baby." Natalie touched Tori's hand, then turned to face Lane. "Literally. And if the father weren't a jerk, that would change everything. It's hard to give up a child—trust me, I know."

"I don't want you getting your hopes up and then Tori changing her mind at the last minute."

"I won't." Tori worked at keeping her voice steady. "I don't have that luxury. I have to keep the baby safe from Russ. That's all I want."

"I've noticed, you say, 'the baby'." Lane's gaze measured Tori—watching her every reaction.

"Once I decided to give the baby up, I stopped saying my."

The doorbell rang.

"I'll get it." Lane stood and strode toward the front of the house.

"You'll have to excuse Lane, he just doesn't want me to get hurt."

"I can understand his point of view." Brant squeezed Tori's hand. "I don't want Tori getting hurt."

Tori's gaze pinged to meet his. Lane worried about Natalie because he loved her. Did Brant have feelings for Tori? More than friend feelings?

Lane came back with a little girl in his arms and a woman following them.

"Hannah? Star?" Natalie stood and hurried to the little girl. "Is something wrong?"

"Sissy Nessa got sick." The little girl scrunched her nose. "It was gross."

Natalie's daughter. And Tori had seen the woman in the store. Must be Hannah's stepmom.

"I don't want Hannah to get it, so I thought I should bring her over." The woman set a backpack in a chair and tousled the child's hair. "Sorry about this, Hannah. But Daddy will come get you as soon as Vanessa gets well."

"Okay."

"Sorry to interrupt." Star turned away.

"I'll walk you out." Lane winked at Natalie. "And then I'll take Hannah to the kitchen."

As the room cleared, Natalie reclaimed her seat. "I'm so sorry for the interruption."

"It's fine." Tori just wanted all the interruptions to go away, so they could get this settled.

"Maybe we should all do some thinking, anyway." Natalie shrugged. "And some praying."

"I get the feeling Lane isn't sold on the idea of adoption." Tori stood.

"Trust me, Lane loves Hannah as if she were his own. I wish she was." Natalie closed her eyes. "But him raising someone's else's child is no problem. He's just scared things will fall through."

"Y'all talk about it and call me." Tori stood up and headed for the front of the house with Brant close behind.

"I will." Natalie followed. "Thanks for coming."

Brant ushered Tori out the door and Natalie closed it behind them.

"Well I'm thoroughly confused about what any of this has to do with Star and her daughters," Brant said.

"You know Star?"

"Her husband, Wyatt, is a bull rider. Hannah and Vanessa are their daughters."

As they trekked back down the driveway, Tori kicked at the gravel, spewing several missiles. "Hannah is Natalie's daughter with Wyatt. Natalie and Wyatt happened before he met Star and they were never married. Natalie was a different person then and she gave Wyatt custody of Hannah. But since she turned her life around, she's part of Hannah's life now."

"Sounds complicated." He matched her stride. "I don't know about this adoption thing."

"Me neither."

He gently grabbed her arm and turned her to face him. "You don't?"

"I'm sure about giving the baby up. I'm just not sure that Natalie and Lane are on the same page."

Her ringtone started up—"Done." Her face warmed. "It's kind of a reminder." DONE with men. And she needed the reminder when Brant was around.

"Who is it?"

"Aunt Loretta." She pressed a button. "Hello?"

"Tori." Her aunt's voice sounded strained.

"What's wrong?"

"Are you alone?"

"No. Brant's with me. Why?"

"I'm afraid it's your daddy. His lawyer called me—I guess because I was your legal guardian. Your daddy passed away this morning, honey."

Her insides twisted. "I'll be there soon." She hung up.

"What's wrong?" Brant gently gripped her shoulders. "You look like you're about to fall over."

"My dad. He um…he died."

"Oh, sweetie." Brant pulled her into his arms.

Her insides tossed and turned, but her eyes stayed dry. She'd hated her father in the past. And wished he'd die back when her mother was still alive. And now, now that he'd been out of her life for years, now that it didn't matter one way or the other if he was alive or dead, he was dead. How did she feel about that? She was a Christian now. Shouldn't she feel something? Like sadness?

Unless something had changed, her dad was burning in torment in hell right now. Where he belonged. Had she really just thought that? Should she be glad someone was in hell? All she felt was bitterness as her stomach continued to roil. She pushed away from Brant.

"I think I'm gonna be sick." She fell to her knees.

Right there in Natalie's front yard, she puked her guts out while Brant held her hair. Again.

A shade of gray. Tori had been a shade of gray since she'd gotten the news.

Brant sat across from her at her aunt's kitchen table. Her hands cupped around her coffee mug, while Aunt Loretta bustled around putting away food neighbors had brought. The house was on the small side and earlier it had been almost standing room only with casserole-bearing church folks.

News traveled fast. Especially when it made the national news. What would it feel like to have your parent's drug overdose all over the news?

He touched her hand. Cold despite the heat of the mug. "You okay?"

"I don't know." She shook her head.

"You should probably eat something. Want me to make a McDonald's run?"

At least that got a slight grin out of her. "No. I'm fine."

"Are you supposed to drink coffee? It seems like when Raquel was pregnant, her doctor cautioned her about coffee."

"I can have one or two cups a day. This is my first."

"How about some meatloaf, butter beans and shoepeg corn casserole," Aunt Loretta suggested.

"Yum." Tori perked up. "Why don't you make my mouth water?"

"I'll have it ready in a jiff. I already got your room ready and I'll get the guest room ready for Brant in a bit."

"Oh, I'm not staying. I'll drive home a little later."

"Nonsense." Aunt Loretta waved her hand through the air as if waving away any protests he might make. "I love company and we've got room. What kind of aunt would I be if I sent Tori's fella home when she's hurting?"

"Aunt Loretta! Brant is not my fella."

"Okay, friend." Aunt Loretta rolled her eyes. "If that's how you wanna play it. Anyway, just stay here. Tori's dam is gonna bust eventually." She clattered pans together as she dug through a cabinet. "Slim may have been a worthless, drunken wife-beater, but he was still Tori's daddy. She'll need a *friend* close."

"It's up to Tori."

"I would like you to stay. Unless you have something else you need to do."

"No rodeo until tomorrow night. I guess I'm all yours."

"But—" Aunt Loretta propped her hands on her hips "—no shenanigans. Not in my house."

Brant's face heated.

Tori's jaw dropped. "We don't…shenanigan. Brant's a Christian. And so am I."

"I know. But in this day and age young folks shack up while they claim the name of Jesus." Aunt Loretta shook her head. "It ain't right. But I'm glad to know y'all know that."

"Besides, what man in his right mind would want to shenanigan with a woman almost six months pregnant with another man's child?" Tori laughed.

Oh, he'd gladly shenanigan with her. Mind out of the gutter, McConnell.

Tori's laughter turned high-pitched and then the tears came.

Brant knelt beside her and she soaked his shoulder once more.

Aunt Loretta patted her back. "Yep, the dam broke. Once she gets calmed down, we'll get some food down her and then you take her for a walk, will ya, Brant? Her color's all off and fresh evening air works wonders."

"I don't know that she's up for a walk." Brant felt every sob in his soul.

"I'm fine." Tori pushed away from him and mopped her face with her paper napkin. "A walk sounds great. Just let me eat and then we'll go."

The scents of onion, tomato and beef filled the small kitchen.

"The glories of the microwave." Aunt Loretta set a plate in front of each of them. "I don't know how we women ever did without it. Bless the food, will ya, Brant?"

"Sure." He bowed his head and heard Tori set her fork down. "Dear Lord, thank you for this food and for bringing my new friends Tori and Aunt Loretta into my life. Give Tori strength to get through the coming days and give her peace about her dad. In Jesus name, Amen."

Probably shouldn't have lied in his prayer. A prayer was supposed to be from the heart. And there was nothing friendly in his heart toward Tori.

Why did Brant make her feel so safe? So comfortable? She leaned into his side, completely content as they trekked the gravel road. "I couldn't have gotten through today without you."

"I didn't do anything. A little driving, a little holding together—that's all."

The late July sun blasted down on them as it began to set. But here with Brant, despite the heat, she wished the evening could last forever.

"I'm not even sure how I feel about my dad's death. What does that say about me?"

"I think it says a lot about him. You don't automatically get love and people to grieve over you. You have to earn it. And from what I hear, he didn't."

"I hated him when I was a kid. Especially when he hit my mom. But he was my father. And deep down somewhere inside, I did love him." Her voice cracked. "I longed for a close, normal relationship with him. And now I'll never have it. I think that's what I'm sad about, that since he's gone, I'll never have the relationship I wanted with him."

Brant pulled her closer against his side. "You're allowed to feel however you feel. You can be sad or mad or glad."

"Are you a mind-reader?"

"Not that I know of. Why?"

"When Aunt Loretta called and told me, one of my first thoughts was that he was probably in hell and he deserved to be there."

"We all deserve to be there. Some more than others."

"You don't deserve to be there."

"I'm no saint. I've got my faults."

"Like…"

"I'm stubborn, determined to get my own way, and I've got a bit of a temper."

"You?"

"Like I said, we all deserve to be in hell. But by choosing Christ, we get a get out of hell free card."

A comfortable silence settled over them. An owl hooted and dogs barked in the distance. She'd never been comfortable with a man without talking or being intimate.

"When's the last time you talked to your dad?" His breath stirred the hair at her temple.

"When I was sixteen." Memories of the scene with Kenny the drummer surfaced. Her dad catching them in Kenny's bed—the things he'd called her. "After I went on the road with him, we had a disagreement and he sent me to live with Aunt Loretta. I hadn't heard from him or seen him since."

"That's twelve years ago. He never called to check on you. Not once?"

"Nope." She shook her head. "Aunt Loretta took him to court and made him pay child support—because she thought I deserved some of his money. He didn't show up, but he agreed to pay. That's how I was able to go to design school."

"I'm sorry, Tori. You deserved better."

Something skittered into the brush along the roadside and she jumped.

"Probably a rabbit." His arm tightened around her. "I mean it. Your father missed out by not spending time with you."

"You really think so?"

"I know so. You're an awesome person, Tori. Anyone would be privileged to know you, to spend time with you."

"Thanks." Her voice cracked. Please not the water works again. But despite her determination to overcome her emotions, her eyes swam.

He patted his shoulder and she sank into him. "I've never cried this much in my life. Jenna says it's pregnancy emotions. Poor Caitlyn's in the same shape."

"I don't mind having a beautiful redhead in my arms. You can cry on me any time."

And she could get used to being in his arms. Who was she kidding? She already was used to it.

The funeral turned out to be a who's who of Country music stars. Brant scanned the faces at the security-detailed cemetery. Even Garrett had flown in on the red-eye to be here for Tori and would fly out immediately after the service to continue his tour. Nashville definitely supported their own. A fan would have a heyday. And a few had tried to sneak in to the private service.

Tori looked like you could knock her over with dandelion fluff and he offered his arm. She clung to him, accepting hug after hug with a tired smile. It was surreal seeing faces he'd only seen on album covers here at the cemetery, offering Tori their condolences, with the hot afternoon rays beating down on them.

"We should get you home," he whispered. "I can tell by looking at you, you're exhausted."

"Gee thanks."

"You're still beautiful. Even when you're exhausted. But I think you and the baby could use some rest."

"You're right." A man's voice.

Brant looked up. A man with sandy-colored hair and brown eyes stared at Tori.

All color had drained from her face. "Kenny."

"It's good to see you. All settled down and pregnant. Marriage suits you. You look great."

"Thanks. But—"

"Brant McConnell." Brant offered his hand.

"Nice to meet you." Kenny clasped his hand. "Kenny James. Well, you should listen to your husband. Go home, get some rest. It was good seeing you. Despite the circumstances."

"You, too."

Kenny gave her an awkward hug and turned away.

"He was my dad's drummer," she whispered. "And my first…boyfriend."

First guy she'd ever slept with. Brant knew it—all the way down to the tips of his cowboy boots. His gaze locked on Kenny's retreating back. With everything in him, he wanted to waylay Kenny from behind and beat him to a pulp. He imagined rolling around in the dirt of the cemetery with fists flying.

He mentally shook himself out of the fantasy. "Come on, let's get you home."

She clung to his arm as they trekked the parched earth to the parking area.

All day people had assumed he was her husband. She'd tried to protest the first time. But he'd introduced himself, offered his hand and accepted the role.

What did it matter who people thought he was? Why

let these people she'd probably never see again know she was pregnant and unmarried? After the first few, she'd stopped trying to explain. Until Kenny.

Why didn't she want Kenny to think she was married? Because she still had feelings for him?

His gut twisted.

Chapter 12

A week since her dad died. Two days since the funeral. Time for Tori to go home.

She hugged her aunt.

"Thanks for everything." Brant set her suitcases by the front door.

He'd stayed that first night, then been a daily visitor sharing meals with Tori and her aunt. Just checking on her, he said.

"Nothing to thank me for." Aunt Loretta hugged him, then patted Tori's cheeks. "And you, you come stay here any time you want. In fact, you could move right back in with me and I'd be tickled pink."

"I'll take these out and wait in the truck. Take your time." Brant shuffled out and shut the door with the toe of his boot.

"That young man's a keeper—reminds me of my Ben."

"He's a good friend."

"Friend." Aunt Loretta rolled her eyes. "Yeah, right. Now listen, I been needing to tell you something. Your daddy faithfully sent money for you ever since he made me your legal guardian. I made sure you got everything you needed and never spent a penny on myself."

"You were wonderful." Like a second mother and the only constant after her real mother's death. "I don't know what I'd have done without you."

"What you don't know is—it was a lot of money. I squirreled the rest away in savings. I've been waiting until you were grown and responsible to tell you."

Tori had never thought of any money being left over. She'd assumed her dad had only sent enough to cover her needs. "Did the court set up the amount?"

"Yes. But your daddy paid more. A lot more."

"Why?"

"I imagine he knew he'd failed you. Failed your mother and the least he could do was take care of you financially. He was twisted up inside—but he did love you—in his own way."

Her father loved her? If so, he had a strange way of showing it. "I don't really need it. I make good money."

"Regardless, it's your money."

"So how much are we talking about?"

"See for yourself." Aunt Loretta dug around in her apron pocket and handed Tori a bankbook.

Tori flipped the book open. More commas and zeroes than she'd ever imagined. Her jaw dropped and her gaze met her aunt's. "Are you serious?"

"Dead serious." Aunt Loretta grinned. "And on top of that, I talked to your father's attorney. Apparently, he had a good accountant who made some good investments. Since you're the only heir, you should get a sizeable inheritance, plus his house in Nashville. You and your baby should never have to worry about anything. In fact, you could quit working and be a stay-at-home mom if you want."

Tori winced. She had to tell Aunt Loretta about the adoption soon.

"Or go into clothing design like you always wanted. You've been designing your own clothes and getting compliments for years. You could even start your own line."

Start her own line. Get her own place. Stand on her own two feet.

"Thank you for taking care of me so well." Tori closed

the bankbook and slid it into her purse. "I'll write you a check once I get everything sorted."

"You most certainly will not. I don't need to be paid for loving you or taking care of you."

"Simmer down. That's not what I meant. I want to share this with you. You've always lived so simply and I want to do something special for you."

"I don't need a thing. And you will not spend your hard-earned money on me."

"Hard earned? I didn't do anything for it."

"Yes, child. You did. You lived with his fists."

The years of seeing her mother get beat up flashed through her mind. Tending her wounds and finding her that last time. Her eyes singed. Yes, he owed Tori. Owed them both. But it was too late for Mama.

"I just wish I'd known what was going on back then. I'll never understand why you or your mama never told me."

"We were scared of him." Think of something else. She shook the memories off. How could she get Aunt Loretta to share in her newfound fortune?

The simple little house had looked the same for as long as she could remember. The ancient kitchen cabinets. Appliances that hadn't been replaced in at least a dozen years. The too-broken-in flowered couch.

"I know. We could redecorate—add on to the house if you want. You've always wanted a sewing room."

"And that little corner in the guest room suits me fine. This money is yours and I don't want a penny of it."

"I'm redecorating the house, so get ready to pick what you want or I will."

"Stubborn." Aunt Loretta clucked her tongue. "Just like your mama. Lordy, I miss her. Now listen, don't be spending anything on me. Your father's attorney will be contacting you soon. In the meantime, you best git. Not that I'm anxious to be rid of you, but you got a handsome keeper out there waiting for you."

Tori's face warmed. "Friend."

"Whatever." Aunt Loretta gave her another hug and propelled her toward the door.

The relentless early August heat had shoved customer after customer into the store all morning. The bell above the door rang as the last browser exited.

Lunch time lull and Tori was relieved. She could barely concentrate. Last night, she'd sketched her entire winter clothing line right down to all the accessories. Her brain brimmed with what stores she'd market to and where her headquarters would be.

But, how could she have her clothing line and still work in Jenna's store? Quitting was not an option. She couldn't let Jenna down. Not after all Jenna had done for her.

"Tori." Jenna's voice tugged her back.

"Hmm."

"Maybe it's too soon for you to be here. You're so distracted and it's only natural. You just buried your father."

"I'm fine and you are not changing your plans." Tori rearranged a bronze-and-gold-tapestry table runner to catch the light better. "You are flying out this afternoon to meet Garrett for the final leg of his tour. You should have left from the cemetery with him."

"He'll be home next week. I could just stay here."

"No. Absolutely not." Tori wagged a finger at her. "I'm fine. Really. It's just…"

"What?"

"I found out my dad sent a lot of money over the years and I've got a pretty sizeable account. Apparently, his accountant made good investments and I'm waiting to hear from his lawyer. I should be the only heir." Unless he left it all to one of his groupies.

"That's wonderful." Jenna did a little bounce. "You can start your clothing designs like you've always wanted."

"Really?"

"Of course. Why not?"

"I can't leave you in the lurch." She rearranged a unique nature-inspired centerpiece decorated with lotus pods, dried artichokes and pomegranates on the table runner. "You've done so much for me."

"Tori, you've been a great employee."

"I have?"

"You've always been reliable and the only time you weren't, it was Russ's fault. Not yours." Jenna took both of her hands. "But this is my dream. Not yours. Though I hate to lose you, I could never make you stay here when your dream is out there waiting for you."

"Really?"

"Of course."

"But if I leave, how will you ever tour with Garrett or sneak off for weekend visits with him?" Tori rolled her eyes. "Of course my being here kept you home this time."

"Not. Your. Fault." Jenna patted her hand. "When I get back, I'll move Susan up to your position and call the design school for references. Susan will train someone new and you'll start your business."

"But I have no idea where to start."

"Me neither." Jenna picked up the phone. "But I just happen to have a cousin with a clothing store. Caitlyn knows all the designers. With her connections, we can do this."

"We?"

"Of course. I'll help you in any way I can."

"Shouldn't you be leaving for the airport?"

"As soon as I get things rolling for you with Caitlyn."

A knot lodged in Tori's throat. Okay, she had a wonderful mother, but a miserable childhood because of her dad.

She'd lost her mother way too soon and her life had gone off-kilter culminating with Russ. Now she was pregnant and had to give up her baby.

But God had surrounded her with wonderful Christian people—Aunt Loretta, Jenna, Brant. He was giving her a chance at a fresh start. A chance to live her dream.

Thank you, Lord.

Tori was here—at the rodeo again. With him.

The only problem he hadn't considered, she was out there sitting with Natalie. Surely Natalie wouldn't pressure her about the adoption. He still had the nagging instinct that Tori wanted to keep her baby.

The coliseum was bursting tonight. Could be the mid-August heat sent them inside for relief. Or maybe finally, he seemed to be getting his footing and fans had gotten over no longer seeing Garrett perform.

Brant put his heart into his final set for the evening—singing the love song to Tori—his audience of one.

The last notes faded away, the spotlight dimmed and he strode from the arena, kicking clods of dirt as he went. He stomped as much debris off as he could and headed to his dressing room for a fresh dousing of cologne in case the manure had seeped into him. He'd never live it down if he went to sit with Tori, she got a whiff of him and had to hurl.

"Mr. McConnell?" An unfamiliar male voice came from behind him.

Brant turned. "Yes?"

A gray-haired man wearing a Western-style suit and a ten-gallon hat approached him.

"I enjoyed your show." The man offered his hand and Brant clasped it.

"Thanks."

"Tex Conway with Country Road Records. Are you with a label?"

Brant swallowed hard. He knew all about the company. Some of the biggest stars in Country music were signed with that label.

"No, sir."

Tex handed him a business card. "I'm here from Nashville on vacation with my family through next week. But I never mind mixing in a little business. I'd like to talk with you when I get back to my office. Call me and we'll set up an appointment."

No *if you're interested.* Tex probably couldn't imagine him not being interested.

The card looked legit with the company label.

"Sure."

"I'll look forward to it. You have a good evening now, ya hear."

"You, too. And thanks."

Like an automaton, Brant unlocked his dressing room door and stepped inside. It was what he'd hoped for. Just in the wrong genre. His heart had always been in Christian music.

Garrett had taken the indirect route from Country music and almost lost his soul in booze and women. It had taken his almost losing his voice and losing Jenna again to bring him back to Christ. But in the end, he'd realized his dream, signed with a Christian label and started the new genre of Christian Country they'd both always dreamed of.

Could Brant do country music, without the booze and women part? Could he sing and perform music without his heart being in it? Could he eventually transition to Christian Country?

And what about Tori? His heart squeezed and he sank into a chair. Could he convince her to marry him, raise the baby together and go to Nashville with him? Could he drag her and the baby on tours with him?

So far, he hadn't seen any chink in her armor against

musicians. She appreciated him as a friend, she'd leaned on him while adjusting to her dad's death, and she'd cried on his shoulder more than a few times. But did she have any feelings for him? Raquel thought so, but not that he could tell.

Which brought up the biggest question. If there was no future with Tori, could he sign with Country Road and leave her behind?

His heart sank to the pit of his stomach.

Brant's mind had spun as he'd driven Tori home. But not enough to keep him from wanting to kiss her. He'd managed to keep his lips to himself and escort her safely inside.

And then he'd called Garrett. Thank goodness Garrett had gotten back home this weekend. If anyone could understand his dilemma, Garrett could.

Endless miles with the tree-lined fence along each side of the drive leading to Garrett's house testified to the trappings Garrett had earned in Country music. Beyond the fence, horses grazed in the moonlight.

Finally, he pulled in the paved drive at the sprawling house. Even this time of night, the mid August heat was oppressive. The front door opened before he could get to the porch.

Jenna beckoned him inside. "Garrett's out back waiting for you by the pool."

"Sorry to bother you when you just got home and it's so late. I wasn't thinking about it being almost midnight when I called."

"No worries. Since I flew out to meet him a few weeks ago, we're both wound up, jetlagged and sleepless. But tomorrow's Saturday."

The house was immaculate. Jenna's professional decorating touch—from the tiled floor with Texas lone star accents to the carefully chosen furnishings and accessories, all with a Western flair that suited Garrett perfectly.

Nothing like Jenna's former house when he and Raquel had first moved in—all silks and satins in different shades of cream and gold froufrou. It must almost hurt her to live in Garrett's house. But she didn't seem to mind. Now that was love.

If only he could have a self-sacrificing love like that with Tori.

Jenna ushered him out the patio door. "Can I get you anything? Coffee, tea, water?"

"I'm fine."

"Hey, Garrett was supposed to invite you to his homecoming celebration lunch tomorrow. He did, didn't he?"

"He did and I'm coming."

"Great. Bring that sister of yours."

"I'll try, but she hasn't found a babysitter around here yet."

"I'd say bring Hunter along, but all mamas need a break sometimes. Try Durlene Warren, Clay's mom. I'll write down her number for you." Jenna waved and went back inside.

"What's on your mind?" Garrett sprawled in a cushioned lounge chair and gestured to the one beside him.

"Tex Conway gave me his business card tonight." Brant relaxed into a chair. The moonlight glistened on the slightly rippling pool water.

"Country Road Records?"

"Yep."

"What are you gonna do?"

"I don't know. He's on vacation through next week. But he wants me to call him."

"So you're torn. Country music was never your dream, but you're tempted because it might be your opportunity to crossover into Christian Country. But you saw what Country music did to me."

"I knew you'd understand."

"First of all, Country music didn't do anything to me. I did it to myself." Garrett played with his wedding band twisting it around and around on his finger. "I was heartsick over my breakup with Jenna and I fell into bed with my manager because I was weak. After that, I felt so guilty, I went into a downward spiral and tried to drown my guilt and missing Jenna in alcohol and every woman I could find."

"So that's how it happened. I always wondered what got you so far off track since I knew you were a Christian."

"Not a very good one. Obviously." Garrett ran a hand through his hair. "But, you don't have to follow in my messed-up footsteps just because you sign a Country music contract. For one thing, you're not heartsick."

"I wouldn't exactly say that."

"Really?" Garrett waggled his eyebrows. "Tori?"

"Guilty."

"How does she feel about you?"

"She thinks I'm a great friend." His chest squeezed. "Ouch."

"Yeah." The high-pitched whir of cicadas made his situation seem more desperate. "But back to Country music."

"Okay, second point. Just because I started in Country and ended up in Christian music doesn't mean you can make the same transition. My new label went out on a limb in launching a new genre with me."

"And since Christian Country is so new, there may not be room for more artists in the genre."

"Yet. But, you need to decide—can you put your heart and soul into Country music and be happy if the opportunity never arises for you to transition to Christian Country?"

The only time his heart had been into singing Country

music over the past several months was the two times Tori had been at the rodeo. "I don't know."

"You need to know before you set up a meeting with Tex Conway. And since you shed new spotlight on the subject—you need to find out how Tori feels about you. If she has feelings for you, you need to find out if she'll go with you on the Country music roller coaster and see where it takes you. And if she won't, can you leave her behind?"

"And if she has no feelings for me—" Brant winced "—can I leave her behind?"

"Ouch again."

"Yeah." Brant stood. "It's late and you have a beautiful wife waiting for you."

"While you just have a beautiful friend."

"You don't have to rub it in."

"That's not what I meant." Garrett walked him to the patio. "If I'd been more patient with Jenna way back when, maybe she'd have married me and gone to Nashville with me. Or maybe I'd have waited for my career until the industry was ripe for a new genre. Maybe all those horrible years and horrible decisions I made would have never happened."

"Trust me—there's some do-overs I wish I could have. But what does that have to do with my beautiful friend?"

"You need to find out how Tori feels about you. If she really thinks of you as only a friend, you need to see if you can change her mind. Love is too rare and precious to let a chance at it slip away."

"Wow." Brant whistled. "You've gone really soft. It must have been singing all those sappy love songs."

"No—it's Jenna." Garrett chuckled. "Tell anybody and I'll ruin your career before it ever starts."

"It actually looks good on you. I'm glad you and Jenna worked things out."

"Me, too. Now go work things out with Tori. She needs someone solid."

"Thanks for the advice."

"Any time."

Brant walked to his truck. What if Tori only saw him as a friend? Could he change her mind? If she didn't have any feelings for him, could he convince her to marry him and let him raise her child anyway? Would she go to Nashville with him? Could he go without her?

Garrett had been helpful, but Brant still had no clue what to do about Nashville. But he did know what to do with Tori.

More than likely, she'd be at the lunch tomorrow since it seemed Jenna wanted them together as badly as Brant did.

Whether she came or not, tomorrow he'd learn how she felt about him. Could his heart take the truth?

His chest tightened.

Chapter 13

The pool begged Tori to jump in instead of merely dangling her bare feet in. The cool water lapped gently against her ankles. Natalie sat beside her, so they could talk before Jenna's other lunch guests arrived.

On the far end of the pool, Garrett and Lane fired up the grill.

"We've made a decision." Natalie swayed her feet back and forth in the water with her face tipped back toward the sun.

"And?"

"Once your baby is born, if he or she needs a home, we'll provide one. No pressure. We're not going to depend on it. So if you change your mind, you're free to raise your baby."

"I won't change my mind." A hard knot formed in her throat.

"I know you think that. But when I had Hannah, my life was a mess and I only thought of her as a complication. But after carrying her for nine months, giving birth to her and hearing her cry, everything changed." Natalie's voice broke. "I refused to see her because I was afraid I'd want to keep her. I'd already signed the papers to give her to Wyatt and I thought I could get on with my life."

"It didn't work out that way?"

Natalie shook her head. "I moved to Garland, but all I did was think about her. I dreamed about her. I heard her crying. I couldn't concentrate and could barely function. She was eighteen months old when I finally gave up trying to forget her."

"Did you fight for custody?"

"No. Maybe I could have, I'm not sure. But by then, I'd done some changing and wanted to do what was best for her. She knows who I am, and Wyatt and I have a loose schedule with her. But she lives with him and Star."

A loud buzz sounded. The buzzer at the gate. More guests.

"Listen." Natalie patted her arm. "I don't want you to go into labor and give birth feeling like there's a wolf at the end of your bed. You need to make the right decision for your baby. And for you. Just let us know what you decide once the baby is born. We're good either way."

"And Lane's okay with this agreement?"

"Yes. We've both done a lot of praying about it."

Tension rolled off Tori's shoulders. Her baby had somewhere to go now.

The door opened and Jenna called. "We good out here?"

"Yes." Natalie pulled her feet from the water and stood. "The rest of our guests have arrived."

Tori started to stand and someone handed her a towel. Her gaze trailed up the male hand and arm. Brant. She hadn't known he was coming.

"Dry those feet. No pregnant women falling in the pool."

"Thanks." Tori dried her feet and he offered his hand to help her up. She took the offer. The heaviness of the baby made her awkward these days. And she still had three months to go.

Raquel, Caitlyn and Mitch joined the gathering.

"So how's your new clothing line coming along?" Caitlyn asked Tori.

"I met with some of the suppliers you introduced to me

and I've already got orders, plus I found a retail space and a factory. I guess I'm waiting on the will to see exactly what I've got to work with."

"You're starting a clothing design company?" Brant frowned.

"Yeah. I found out my dad left me some money, so I'm going for it."

"It's been Tori's dream ever since I've known her." Jenna set the nearby table.

"That's great." Raquel turned to Jenna. "And thanks for the scoop on the babysitter. Durlene is great—Hunter took right to her."

"Durlene's been helping Aubrey raise kids as long as I can remember." Mitch settled in one of the lounge chairs. "She's my aunt, but she was my babysitter, too."

A loud buzz sounded.

"I wonder who that is. All our guests are here." Jenna hurried over and pressed a button by the back door. "Yes?"

"It's Desiree."

Jenna's eyes widened.

And Tori's did too. Desiree as in Desiree Devine. Garrett's long ago Nashville manager who'd shown up at his first Christian concert and caused lots of tumult for Jenna and Garrett.

Garrett rushed to his wife's side. "How did you find me, Desiree?" he barked.

"A mutual friend. I know you probably hoped to never see me again. But I'd like to talk to you and Jenna."

"We have guests. Now's not a good time."

"Please. I came to apologize for what I did."

"We'll take that as an apology." Garrett clenched his teeth. "Goodbye, Desiree."

"Please. I can't rest until I apologize to both of you—face-to-face."

Jenna—the queen of giving second chances—put a hand on Garrett's arm. Her eyes pleaded with him.

"All right. But make it fast."

"I'm sorry, everybody." Jenna took Garrett's hand. "But this is important. It shouldn't take long."

"Well I don't know why you'd see her," Natalie huffed.

"Because where would we all be if we hadn't gotten a second chance?"

"We could leave and do this another time." Lane set the metal tongs down. "I haven't put the steaks on the grill yet."

"No." Garrett growled. "She's already ruined my day, but I won't let her ruin our lunch."

Garrett and Jenna headed for the house.

An uncomfortable hush settled over the guests.

Why had Desiree shown up now? Tori wished she could be a fly on the wall. In spite of all the times Jenna had helped her out, Tori couldn't do anything to help Jenna now. Helpless.

Tori pulled into the drive at the guesthouse. How could she be so tired? All she'd done was go to lunch.

Poor Jenna. Even though Desiree had been truthful and only shown up to apologize, the encounter had obviously rattled Jenna. And Garrett worried about Desiree going to the press with the location of his house. Yet after Desiree left, Jenna and Garrett pulled off a chatty, fun lunch.

Tori wanted to be Jenna when she grew up.

Only problem, she and Jenna were the same age, so Tori should be grown up by now.

Designs waited for her all over the house, people to call and orders to take. But all she wanted to do was take a nap. She hauled her hulking body out of the car.

Maybe she'd take a short nap and then get to work.

Probably be more productive that way. She slid her key in the lock. No click. It was already open.

Odd. She could have sworn she locked the door. She always locked the door. Especially since Russ could be lurking around. No, that was ridiculous. She was on a private ranch with an alarm system on the gate. No one could get in. And as far as she knew, he hadn't paid his fine. And if he did get out of prison, Mitch was to be notified.

Deep breath. In and out. Calm down. She turned the knob and pushed the door open, hung her purse on the hook by the door and headed for her bedroom.

A hand clamped over her mouth. Spasms coursed through her and she tried to cry out.

"Hey, babe."

A whiff of alcohol turned her stomach. Russ.

"Just when were you going to tell me I'm about to be a daddy?" His words slurred together.

She stopped struggling against him. That would only make him mad and he might hurt the baby. Besides, it was no use. She was no match for his big bulk.

"Now this is what we're gonna do. I'm gonna move my hand, so we can talk and you're going with me. I've got a new place. It's real nice and you'll like it. If you scream, I'll go get your boyfriend and kill him with my bare hands. If you try to get away, I'll kill your boyfriend, beat that baby right out of you, and kill you too. Got it."

She nodded.

Russ moved his hand.

"How did you get in the gate?"

"Well now, I knew there must be somebody who wants revenge on Garrett Steele bad enough to pay my fine."

"Desiree."

"Busted. She was easy to look up. Since she kind of ruined her reputation as an entertainment agent, she's desperate for a job. Then I saw you at the Stockyards yesterday.

Saw you was holding out on me. So, I followed you. Once I got a load of this place, I figured it had to be Garrett Steele's place and I knew Desiree could get me in."

"I can't believe she went along with this." Her voice came out too high.

"All I had to do was promise her a piece of dear old daddy's pie. I figure you've got plenty of funds for all of us."

"So that's what this is about. Money."

He backhanded her across the mouth.

Her head flew back and her body followed. She curled her arms around the baby and landed hard against the side of the couch. She tasted the iron of her own blood and wretched on the floor.

"Look at the mess you made. Now get up, slut. Enough talk. Let's move."

She had to do exactly what he said. And not make him mad. He'd hurt the baby without a second thought. If he hadn't already.

But she had to get away. Going with him and trying to keep him happy hadn't worked before. And it wouldn't work now. Something would always set him off and he'd take it out on her. And the baby. She couldn't let that happen.

She pushed awkwardly to her feet. He didn't help. Nothing like Brant—not a speck of gentleness in Russ. She wiped at her mouth. Bleeding pretty badly.

If he'd let her go to the bathroom, maybe she could squeeze out the window and make it to her car.

"Can I go to the bathroom and wash my mouth? Maybe brush my teeth?"

"Only because I don't wanna have to smell your breath. But I'm going with you, so's you don't get any ideas." Russ wrenched her arm behind her back.

Don't cry out. For some reason that always made him madder. She cleaned up her tender mouth as best she could with one hand, not really caring since Russ hadn't fallen for her escape ruse.

He dragged her out the door and toward his truck.

"Let me drive. You've been drinking."

"Nice try." He shoved her in the passenger side.

As he rounded the truck, she considered jumping out. But she couldn't run fast enough to get away from him. Especially not with the extra weight of the baby. And *if* she made it back to the house and locked herself inside, he'd break a window and come in after her. Then he'd kill Brant. She didn't doubt him—not one bit.

She'd wait until he drove into a populated area. Then she'd think of something.

Please Lord, don't let him wreck us.

The trees lining the endless fence blurred together as Brant made the long drive back to the highway from Garrett's ranch.

Strange lunch, but in the end it had gone as planned after Desiree did her apologizing and left.

Brant had enjoyed being with Tori as usual. But her new business venture knocked the wind out of him. And she'd slipped out without him even realizing it until he saw her car gone.

How could she go to Nashville with him—if he went— if she had a business to run? And how could he ask her to give up her dream to go with him—if he went? How had their dreams managed to come between them? Just like Jenna and Garrett. Their dreams had kept them apart for years—until they'd finally reached a compromise.

The difference—he had no idea how Tori felt about him.

A hard knot settled in his chest. He needed to know.

Brant turned down her road. Maybe he could live in Aubrey and have his career. In between tours, he could live happily ever after with Tori. For the first several years, he'd be on the road a lot. But once he got his career established, he could cut back like Garrett.

Until then, maybe Tori could go with him. If he convinced her to keep her baby, they wouldn't have to worry about school for a while. And she could put together clothing designs from anywhere.

If she loved him.

A truck appeared in the distance. Tori drove a car. Who would be visiting her? For all he knew, she might be seeing someone. Like that Kenny guy from her dad's funeral. The truck neared and he didn't recognize it. A man driving too fast. Familiar. Brant focused on the passenger side as the two trucks met. Tori.

And he remembered where he'd seen the man. At Jenna's store and in court. Russ.

Brant slammed on his break and spun gravel in a U-turn.

Mitch was still at Garrett's. Brant grabbed his phone from the seat and jabbed his address list button, then the *G*. Garrett's number popped up and he pushed the call button.

"Hello?" Jenna's cheery voice came over the line.

"Is Mitch still there?"

"Sure, he's right…"

"Russ has Tori."

"Oh no. How? When did he get out? Russ has Tori, Mitch."

"I'm following them. We're still on the ranch drive, but he's getting near the gate."

"Mitch is on his way. Garrett's calling 911."

He tried to catch up with Russ. But he didn't want to make Russ go any faster. Not with precious cargo in the passenger seat.

Russ neared the gate and didn't slow.

"Open the gate, Jenna," Brant shouted.

"No. He'll get away with Tori."

"He's gonna crash into it. Open the gate."

"I opened it." Jenna's voice cracked. "Oh, dear Lord, keep Tori safe."

The iron gate slid ever so slowly open as Russ blasted toward it. He barely cleared it and tires squealed as he turned toward Denton.

"He's headed toward Denton."

"I'll give Mitch your number."

Brant ended the call and hung back—far enough to keep an eye on Russ's truck—hoping he'd slow down.

A truck came roaring up behind him. Mitch.

His phone rang and he grabbed it. "Hello?"

"It's Mitch. I'm assuming you're staying back to keep him from getting reckless."

"Yes."

"Here's what I want you to do. There's a nice straight stretch coming up. I want you to pull over and raise your hood. He'll think you're having truck trouble and he's in the clear. I'll stay with him after that and we'll have the advantage since he won't know the Texas Rangers are onto him just yet. I've got backup heading him off."

"Okay." Everything in him screamed not to let her out of his sight. The straight stretch loomed in front of him. Against everything in him, Brant pulled over, jumped out and lifted his hood.

"Good job."

"When we get closer to town, I'll take advantage of the first stoplight and get her out of there. Brant?"

"Yeah."

"I want you to go home. This could get ugly. Do you know if he has a weapon?"

"I have no clue."

"I don't need any civilians in the line of fire. Just stay clear and I'll let you know when we've got her."

"Just keep her safe."

The line went dead. Brant's heart would surely explode. He got back in his truck.

And pulled back onto the highway. Within minutes, Mitch's truck was in sight.

His phone rang again and he grabbed it.

"McConnell!" Mitch barked. "What part of stay clear did you not understand?"

"I can't."

"Do I need to have you arrested for obstruction of justice?"

"Tell me something, Mitch! If Caitlyn was in that truck and you weren't a Texas Ranger, where would you be?"

Silence for a few seconds. "Checkmate. Just stay out of our way."

"It's a good thing your boyfriend's truck broke down." Russ snickered. "He was making my trigger finger itch."

The gun lay in his lap.

Hopelessness threatened to overwhelm Tori. Brant wasn't behind them anymore. At least he was safe. He'd probably called the police long ago. But where were they?

At least Russ hadn't lost control of the truck.

If she waited 'til they got to Denton and the light happened to be red, she could jump out and get help. But Russ might start shooting. She couldn't risk that. For the baby or for innocent bystanders.

There was a wooded area close to the road coming up. That might work.

She clasped a hand over her mouth. "I'm gonna be sick again."

"Hold it in."

"I can't." She wailed and threw in a fake gag.

"Not in my truck, you don't." Russ didn't slow enough and bounced the truck onto the grassy shoulder.

If she had really been sick, she'd have lost it.

As soon as the truck stopped, she bailed out and ran into the woods.

Russ spewed curse words and his truck door slammed.

Panic coursed through her. She couldn't outrun him. And Brant was gone. She had to save herself. For the baby's sake. A large branch lay on the ground and she slowed enough to grab it.

"I see you, Tori. You can't get away from me. Ever."

A siren screeched in the distance.

Footfalls crashed through the brush behind her. Closer than before.

Never in her life had she ever hit anyone. But she had to. This was life-or-death. For her baby.

She spun around and swung the branch like a club. It made contact with the side of Russ's skull with a sickening thud.

He groaned and went down, slurring curse words as he grabbed his bleeding head.

She wheeled back toward the highway. If she could just get to his truck before he caught up with her.

But what if he had the keys? Still the highway was her best chance. Surely someone else would come along and help her. They were near Denton and she could hear traffic.

Footfalls behind her again. Gaining on her.

His arm came around her middle and his hand clamped over her mouth. She swung the club back over her head.

"It's me," Brant whispered and took his hand off her mouth. "Where's Russ?"

She stilled and leaned into him, trembling. "Behind us somewhere. I hit him and he fell."

He grabbed her hand and ran toward the highway. The sirens blared now and blue lights flashed.

"Put your hands up, so they'll know we're not the bad guys."

With both their hands up, they stepped out of the woods. Half a dozen police cars lined the road and all guns turned on them.

A chill ran down Tori's spine.

"I'm Brant McConnell and this is Tori Eaton. Russ Dawson was holding her hostage. He's in the woods, along with Mitch Warren."

"At ease," one of the officers shouted and the guns lowered.

Tori blew out a big breath.

"Is Dawson armed?"

"Yes, he has a handgun."

"Get in my cruiser and stay there."

Brant supported Tori as she stepped across the steep ditch.

"You can't get away from me," Russ shouted as they approached the police car, and a blast came from behind them.

Chapter 14

Gunshots rang out and Brant tackled Tori, doing his best to cradle her gently to the ground and cover her body with his.

Shots fired back and forth until it all became one giant, seemingly endless explosion, and Tori screamed until it stopped. Tires squealed away and several answered in pursuit. Silence.

"We're clear," Mitch shouted. "He got away, but we're in pursuit. Y'all okay?"

"I think so." Brant rolled off her. "Sorry about that. I was trying to keep you safe."

"It's okay." Her voice trembled.

"Did he hurt you? The baby?"

"I think we're okay. What were you doing in the woods?"

"Saving you. How did you end up in the woods?"

"I was saving myself."

Mitch crouched beside them to examine Tori. "With the pregnancy, I think we should have a doctor check Tori out and then I'll need to get a statement from her."

"I'll take her to the E.R." Brant helped her up and walked her to his truck.

"I'll give you an escort." Mitch got in his truck and set his siren on top.

"There's blood on your skirt." Panic rang in Brant's tone.

"It's from my lip. The baby seems to be fine. I'm not

cramping or anything." She leaned into him. "I was so scared he was going to hurt the baby. Or you."

"Me?"

"He saw me at the Stockyards. He must have seen us together. He said if I screamed or tried to get away, he'd kill you."

"They'll get him. Don't worry. And he should go to prison for a while since he fired shots at officers. I'm just sorry he hurt you again." He propped her against his truck and gently dabbed at her battered mouth with a handkerchief.

"I must be a sight."

Her stomach kept him at a slight distance. But not far enough.

"A beautiful sight." One he couldn't resist anymore. He rained kisses over her forehead, nose and eyes tasting her tears, then pulled back enough to look at her.

She opened her eyes and his gaze strayed to her mouth. Her chin tipped up.

And he needed no further invitation. Brant claimed her lips, tasting all their sweetness. "Ouch."

"Oh, sorry." He brushed a gentle kiss on the uninjured side of her lips, then opened his truck door, and helped her climb up.

If he ever got his hands on Russ Dawson...

At least a dozen fluffy pillows cushioned Tori's back in the king-size bed. Jenna had insisted she spend the night. Even though the doctor had said she and the baby were fine and prescribed rest for a couple of days. Even though Garrett had hired one of his bodyguards to permanently man the gate. But no word on Russ yet.

And with everything that had happened and Russ still out there somewhere, all Tori could think about was the kiss. Brant had kissed her. What did that mean?

A knock sounded at the door.

"Tori. You awake?" Jenna whispered.

Like she could sleep after that kiss. But Jenna didn't know that part. "Sure. Come on in."

The door opened and Jenna perched on the foot of her bed. "Mitch called. Russ wrecked his truck fleeing the police. He's in the hospital—pretty bunged up—but alive."

Tori hugged her stomach. She probably shouldn't feel relieved that Russ was injured. But it would keep him from hurting her and the baby again.

"And you have a visitor. Brant is here. Are you up to seeing him?"

Was she? She definitely wanted to see him. But it would be awkward—after the kiss. "Sure."

"Okay." Jenna squeezed her foot. "I'll send him in."

Tori practiced not hyperventilating as Jenna left. Heavy footfalls in the hall. And Brant stepped into the room. Head down, his eyes on the floor.

What was with the hangdog thing? Not like Mr. Take Charge at all.

"I brought you McDonald's."

"It's a good thing I'm a cheap date." She squeezed her eyes closed. Date? Had she really just said that?

Brant scuffed the toe of his boot against the floor, approached her bed and dug each item out of the McDonald's bag. "Think it'll make you sick?"

"No. I've finally gotten to where smells don't bother me." Suddenly famished, she opened the sandwich. "It actually smells great. Want to pray?"

Still without looking at her, Brant took her hand in his and bowed his head. "Dear Lord, thank you for keeping Tori and her baby safe. Thank you for letting Russ end up where he belongs. Thank you for Texas Rangers. And bless this food. Help Tori to have a healthy, happy and safe baby. Amen."

"You think it's okay with God for us to be relieved Russ is in the hospital?"

"No. He wants us to forgive Russ. But that's gonna take some time. At least for me. And I think God understands that." Finally, his gaze met hers, drowning her in jade intensity.

"I guess I shouldn't pray for him to die."

"Probably not." Brant scanned the lace and satin-decked room. "Wow, it's really flowery and girly in here."

She chuckled and took a bite of the Filet-O-Fish. "Oh that's good. How did you know just what I needed?"

"Figured we could all use some comfort about now. I don't know what I'd have done if he'd hurt you. Or the baby."

Her heart thundered. "Maybe that chapter of my life is over. If Russ lives, he'll go to prison. Last time I checked, you can't shoot at Texas Rangers and get away with it."

"You gonna keep the baby?"

"I don't know." She took a swig of her shake. "The only way I could do that is if I felt like Russ would never bother us. Ever. Again."

"Big decision."

"Yeah. And not much time to make it." She patted her bulging stomach.

They fell into silence as she polished off her sandwich and fries, then drained her shake.

"Speaking of decisions, I finally got my rodeo break."

Her heart sank. "Really?"

"A record producer from Nashville saw me perform at the Stockyards. He wants me to meet with him in Nashville."

"To offer you a contract?" Her heart sank further—all the way down to her toes.

"Probably."

"That's awesome." She tried to infuse excitement into her tone.

"It's not what I dreamed of, but it could lead into Christian music like with Garrett. I'd given up on that dream."

"You should never give up on your dreams." Just don't cry. Hold it together until he leaves. She had no right to hold on to him or interfere with his dream. Her gaze dropped to her stomach.

"I've been really torn. I don't want to sing Country music, but can I afford to pass up this chance? And maybe I gave up that dream because I have a new one."

"A megachurch."

"You."

Her gaze flew to his. "Me?"

"I've fallen in love with you, Tori."

Something in her chest exploded into thousands of butterflies. "Me?"

"Yes—you. From your strawberry blond hair to your pregnant belly to your perseverance and strength all packed in a tiny wisp of beauty. The main reason I couldn't decide about Nashville was that I didn't want to leave you."

She wanted to tell him she loved him. With all her heart. But she couldn't keep him from his dream. Besides, he deserved better than her.

"Tori, do you have any feelings for me? I mean other than friendship?" His jade eyes reflected all the love he felt for her. How had she missed his feelings so clearly displayed?

If he'd stop looking at her like that, she could tell a lie. Release him to pursue his dream, to find a woman worthy of him and to never worry about Russ again.

"You passed friendly feelings about the third time you brought me a Filet-O-Fish."

"Really?" Brant pulled her into his arms. "Oh, Tori, I

Shannon Taylor Vannatter 163

want to marry you and raise your baby as my own. I want to have more babies with you."

"Whoa. Wait a minute." She pushed against his chest.

He released her—just enough to look at her. "What?"

"What about Nashville?"

"Today convinced me, I can't leave you. And Nashville was never really my dream. But you are. We'll get married and stay right here. Maybe someday a megachurch will call me and we'll achieve my dream together. That is if it's not far enough away to interfere with your business."

"I think we need to slow down, Brant. I've got a lot of baggage."

"And I love all of it." He kissed the tip of her nose. "Except for Russ, of course. But even if he survives, goes to prison and one day gets out, I can protect you and the baby."

His tender gesture tugged her heart toward surrender.

"But you shouldn't have to. You should end up with some virgin preacher's daughter with no baggage. Not a woman pregnant by an abusive criminal who doesn't even know if she's keeping the baby or not."

He winced and let go of her. "I never claimed to be perfect. And trust me, sadly there are a lot fewer virgin preacher's daughters than you'd think. So you've made some mistakes in the past. So have I. Some of your mistakes have haunted you." He pressed his hand against her belly. "But some turned into blessings. I love you, Tori. I love your baby."

"I think we should slow down and think about things. I need to at least see what happens with Russ. And decide what to do about the baby before I can even begin to entertain the idea of us."

He nodded and drew close again. His gaze latched onto her lips.

She pressed a fingertip against his mouth and shivered.

"That's not a good way to keep a clear head and think about things."

"No. But it's fun and it might sway my case." He mumbled against her finger.

And she shivered again. Strength. It would take a lot of strength to resist him. And she was suddenly too tired to be strong. "I'm tired."

"You look tired. Beautiful, but tired." He cupped her cheek and kissed her forehead. "Sweet dreams and don't forget to think about me. You should probably start planning our wedding." Brant settled in the recliner by her bed. "Mind if I stay a while?"

"Why?"

"Because a maniac stole something I love today and I'm still pretty shaken. I'd like to just sit and look at you for a while."

Her face warmed. "I'm fine. But you can stay. If…"

"If?"

"If you won't make fun of me for snoring or drooling."

"I'd like to watch you snore and drool for the rest of my life."

Pushing pillows aside, she sank into the bed and closed her eyes. How could she relax with Brant staring at her? But all the emotions and physical turmoil had caught up with her. She was exhausted. A heaviness seemed to drag her down and her head went fuzzy.

The "Bridal Chorus," pink roses and satin filled the church. But whose wedding? She looked down. Skinny again—no pregnant stomach. Her flat belly sheathed in white satin. A man in a tuxedo stood at the front of the church with his back toward her. She tried to run to him, but her feet dragged as if in quicksand. Seeming hours passed as she slogged down the aisle. Finally, she made it to the groom and touched his shoulder.

Brant turned to face her, smiling and happy. Safe. And he was holding their baby.

She drowned in his green eyes, but then they turned brown, his hair became blond and his handsome smile turned into Russ's sneer.

"Give me my baby!" she screamed. But Russ only laughed at her. Still holding the baby, he picked Tori up with his other arm and slung her over his shoulder. She beat against his back with both fists and pleaded for someone to help her. But the strangers in the church only laughed.

"Tori." Someone grabbed her shoulder. "Tori. Wake up."

She opened her eyes.

"You were dreaming." Brant hovered close. "Are you okay?"

"Yeah. I'm fine."

"Russ can't hurt you anymore."

For now. But now that he knew she had his baby and she had money—she'd never be free of him. Not even with him in prison. And she couldn't drag Brant into her nightmare.

She had to settle things with Russ before she could even think about a future with Brant.

A lemon. Or a lemon-colored beach ball. Tori smoothed the yellow sundress over the mound of her stomach. She turned from the mirror, grabbed her purse and went to find Jenna.

Garrett and Jenna were in an intense embrace in the great room. Yeah, she definitely needed to get out of here and give the newlyweds their privacy. She tiptoed, trying not to make any noise.

"Ahem." Jenna cleared her throat.

"Sorry about that." Garrett actually blushed. "Just giving my wife a goodbye kiss before she heads off to the store."

"It's your house." Tori shrugged. "You can plaster yourselves together wherever you want. Sorry I interrupted."

"Actually, it's a good thing you did. I need to get going." Jenna grinned that happily-married-living-in-bliss smile of hers. "Where are you going looking so sunshiny? Aren't you supposed to be resting?"

"I've rested for three days." Tori rolled her eyes. "Besides, I've got a meeting with my lawyer and Dad's attorney, then I'm going house hunting." And she was going to see Russ. But they didn't need to know that.

"Oh yeah, I forgot about the attorney. But a house? You can stay in the guesthouse indefinitely."

"I know. Believe me, I so appreciate everything y'all have done. But I need to spread my wings."

"Understandable. And you're safe now." Garrett gave her a stiff hug. "But let us know if we can do anything to help."

"I'll miss you around here." Jenna shrugged. "And at the store."

"How's the new employee?"

"Brittany's great. I've known her forever from church and Natalie helped her out a few years ago. But she's not you."

"That's probably a good thing." Tori laughed at the irony.

"You're an awesome person, Tori." Jenna hugged her. "And I'm proud of you for the turnaround you've made."

"Thanks."

"I'll walk you out."

"Can you give me a ride to my car?"

"Actually, Garrett had one of the ranch hands drive it over here."

"Thanks." She and Jenna trekked to their separate cars. Today, she'd settle things with Russ once and for all.

Then she'd think about Brant. Was it really possible for her and Brant to have the kind of happily-ever-after Jenna shared with Garrett?

Tori's heels clicked down the corridor of the hospital. Wow. She was free—financially. How had her father amassed such a fortune without blowing it all on booze, drugs and women?

She scanned the numbers by each door and found Russ's room. Her feet stalled and she drew in a big breath, then tapped on the slightly ajar door.

No answer. She tentatively stepped into the room.

Wires and monitors surrounded Russ. He was asleep, his face battered and bruised. Small and helpless. Despite everything, she felt sorry for him.

The antiseptic smell of the hospital turned her stomach. Thank goodness she'd finally gotten past getting sick at every little scent.

His eyes opened and his sneer was weaker than usual. "Come to gloat since I'll never walk again?"

"I didn't know and I'm truly sorry. But I came to get you to sign these."

"What is it?" He pushed the button that raised him into a sitting position.

"I had my lawyer draw it up. It's an agreement to relinquish custody rights of our child to me."

"I ain't signing that. Why would I?"

"Look around, Russ, what can you offer a child?" She hated to be so cruel, but she needed to be free of him. Once and for all.

He visibly shrank. "Nothing, I guess, but that baby's still mine. And there's nothing you can do to deny it." He frowned. "Unless you cheated on me."

"No. I'll have a paternity test if you want." She'd slept around in the past, but she'd been monogamous in each relationship. If they could be called relationships. She shuddered. How had she lived that way?

"Well, I ain't signing nothing."

"How much will this cost you, Russ? How will you pay your hospital bills? I imagine you'll get disability to live on. But what about all of this?" She scanned all the medical equipment surrounding him.

"I'll think of something."

"Maybe we could come to an understanding."

"Like what?" he spat.

"I'll pay your hospital bills and you sign this."

He glared at her. And even though he was in a hospital bed with no use of his legs, a chill crept up her spine.

No, he wouldn't intimidate her. She'd intimidate him. She had the upper hand this time.

She didn't shrink from his glare, but held eye contact, and jiggled the papers at him.

He jerked them out of her hand.

Expecting him to rip the document to shreds, she held her breath.

"Got a pen?" Defeat and desperation echoed in his tone.

She handed him the pen and a heavy burden slipped from her shoulders as she watched him sign the papers.

The baby was hers. She could stop calling her child the baby. *My baby.* And she was keeping her baby.

He handed her the signed document.

"Thank you for doing the right thing, Russ."

"I figured you'd say something like, *That's a first.*"

"I didn't come here to hurt you or rub your situation in. I just want the freedom to raise my baby."

"Good luck, Tori."

The rare tender side of him—it didn't show often and it didn't last long.

"You too, Russ. I'll pray for you."

A confused frown furrowed his brow. "I don't need no prayers."

Oh yes, he did. "Goodbye then." She hurried out the door.

On autopilot, she trekked the long corridor, took the elevator to the ground floor and exited the hospital.

Thank you, Lord. My baby is mine.

She'd call and make arrangements for Russ's bill later.

"Tori?" a woman called as she walked toward the parking lot.

Tori turned around. Raquel, Brant's sister. "Hey."

"I'm glad to see you looking so well after your ordeal. You're not here because of any complications, are you?"

"No. Just visiting someone. Is everything okay with you?" Brant. Was Brant okay?

"Fine. One of the students at school broke his arm on the playground. I thought the friendly face of a nurse he knows might make him feel more at ease."

"That's sweet."

"You know, Brant won't tell me anything about what's going on with y'all. But he's crazy about you, I can tell."

Her insides fluttered. "Really?"

"I'll have to admit—I was leery at first. I mean how many guys fall in love with a woman pregnant with another man's child twice in one lifetime?"

Chapter 15

What? Tori tried not to look as confused as she felt, so Raquel would continue.

"At first I thought he might be trying to make up for what happened with Tiffany—like it was his fault or something. But he really loves you."

Tiffany? Tori's mind reeled.

"But you know, I finally realized he was a kid back then. He'd been in puppy love with Tiffany for years, but she was his best friend's girl. And Brant's not the kind of guy to mess with that. But once Davis got her pregnant and dumped her, Brant felt sorry for her and saw his chance to be her hero."

Raquel shrugged. "Maybe if she hadn't been the preacher's daughter, she wouldn't have been so ashamed. If she hadn't snuck off to have that abortion and she'd lived, I still don't think they'd have made it. Tiffany didn't love him."

"She didn't?"

"Shocking, I know. What kind of girl wouldn't fall in love with my brother?" Raquel waved her hand through the air, as if sweeping the revelation away. "But all of that is past history. It has nothing to do with the way he feels about you. He'd love you whether you were pregnant or not. In fact, he mentioned you might give the baby up—so that's proof—it's not only the baby he loves—it's you."

No. Brant was following his past history. He'd proposed to her because he felt sorry for her. Just like he had Tiffany. But Tiffany had died.

And Tori wouldn't be his stand-in Tiffany.

"Anyway, I better go see my student. It was nice bumping into you."

"You, too." Tori hugged herself. Blinking back tears, she hurried to her car.

She'd still keep her baby. But she didn't need Brant or any other man. She'd raise her child on her own and be the best mom she could be.

Brant slid into his favorite booth at Moms on Main and fiddled with the velvety ring box in his pocket. The early September sun bathed the front windows in light. Tori wanted to meet with him. Surely that meant she had an answer for him. Two painfully slow weeks had passed since he'd told her how he felt and he'd barely seen her since. As if she were avoiding him.

Would she give him the answer he wanted?

If she loved him, would she really have to think about her answer? For two weeks? Maybe she'd asked for time because he'd popped the question right after the ordeal with Russ.

Great romantic timing there, McConnell.

The door opened and he looked up. A man entered the restaurant.

His future hung in the balance over hot fudge sundaes at Moms on Main. Was that a bad sign? She said her feelings turned into more than friendship over his third McDonald's offering. His heart nosedived.

If she planned to say yes, wouldn't she have asked him to meet her at McDonald's? But maybe she'd chosen Moms because it was in Aubrey. Or maybe she didn't need comfort food when she said yes.

Yeah, he liked that scenario.

His phone rang and he slid it out of his pocket. An unfamiliar number. "Hello?"

"Is this Brant McConnell?"

"Yes."

"This is John Peters, senior pastor at The Message in Dallas."

Brant's heart soared. The megachurch he'd applied at a year ago. "It's good to hear from you."

"We'd like to interview you for our new worship leader if you're still interested."

"I'm very interested."

"Could you meet with me next week, say Monday at noon."

"I'll be there." Brant wrote the time and date on a napkin.

"I'll look forward to meeting with you."

Could it really all work out so perfectly? He'd marry Tori, take the Dallas church and they'd live happily ever after.

The door opened again and Tori strode in—a ray of hope in a pretty blue dress. Her gaze scanned the tables and landed on him. No smile—no yes, I'll marry you in her eyes.

A lump the size of her belly settled in Brant's throat as she headed in his direction.

"Hey. Thanks for meeting me."

"I ordered you a sundae—whipped cream and nuts."

She didn't even look at the sundae or sit down. "I can't marry you."

"Don't say that." Brant couldn't hide the pleading in his tone as his dream threatened to die.

"We don't have a future together, Brant."

"How can you say that? Is this something to do with that nightmare you had? You can't base our future on a nightmare. Russ can't hurt you anymore."

"No, he can't. He's paralyzed from the waist down—permanently."

Brant's heart did a little giddyup. "God forgive me, but that's perfect. He can't hurt you or anyone else now."

"I had the same reaction. He signed his custody rights over to me. The baby and I are both safe. You're free to pursue your dream." She turned and walked away.

Leaving his heart trampled on the floor. Leaving him to watch her sundae melt. Along with all his dreams.

But she'd admitted her feelings for him. He couldn't just sit here.

"Tori! Wait!" Brant called after her.

She closed her eyes. She'd almost made it to her car. Almost escaped.

If she looked at him again, could she continue to resist?

"Why?" He was right behind her now.

No choice but to face him. Steeling all her resolve, she turned around. "We're too different. Our dreams are different. We were never meant to be. And I can't hold you back from Nashville."

"I turned Nashville down. Not because of you, but because it's not what I want." His hands gently settled on her upper arms.

And some of her resolve dissolved at his touch.

"I applied at a megachurch in Dallas last year. They called me a little while ago and I have an interview Monday. If it works out, I'll be the worship leader there. It's not too far of a commute. We'll get married and live right here in Aubrey." He fished in his pocket and pulled out a black velvet box. "I'll adopt your baby and we'll be a family."

Tori couldn't tear her eyes away as he opened the box to reveal a glittering marquis. Everything she'd ever dreamed of and thought impossible. A gentle, caring man with the perfect diamond, the perfect life, the perfect love. And with everything in her, she wanted to say yes.

But it wasn't perfect. She couldn't slip into the life he'd wanted with Tiffany. She wouldn't be a substitute. And neither would her baby.

"I'm keeping my baby, but I'm raising him or her on my own."

He opened his mouth, then clamped it shut and gave her a defeated nod.

She turned away as her eyes filled with tears. The only chance she'd ever had at happiness and she'd walked away. She got in her car and clamped her fist to her mouth to muffle the sobs.

At least she didn't have to drive far. And since she was an emotional mess, she might as well stop to see Natalie and break the news.

"You said you were coming by to talk." Garrett urged his palomino to a trot then eased into a stride beside Brant's bay. "But all you've done so far is silently brood."

"A month ago, I thought I was going to lose her." Brant kept his gaze on the open pasture. Mid-September. Still in the nineties, the cracked, parched earth dotted with tufts of hardy grasses and weeds cried out for rain.

The way his heart cried out for Tori.

"When I saw her in that maniac's truck." He cleared his throat. "It put everything in perspective. I decided not to go to Nashville. It's not what I want."

"What do you want?"

"Tori. I proposed to her."

"Wow."

"She turned me down." Just saying it out loud sent a hot knife slicing through his heart.

"Dealing with someone like Russ could skew a person's perspective." Garrett scanned the cloudless horizon. "She's had a big month. Let her adrenalin settle and maybe she'll change her mind."

"I don't think so. Maybe I should go to Nashville. Tex Conway said to call if I change my mind. Or maybe Dallas. There's obviously nothing for me here."

"Dallas?"

"I got an offer from a megachurch."

Silence ruled for several minutes. "One question?"

"What?"

"Why did you move here?"

"To be closer to Raquel and Hunter, to take the Stockyards gig and to be the song leader at church."

"And all of that is still here. Tori isn't the reason you came to Aubrey. You didn't even know her until you got here."

"How'd you get so smart?"

"I guess Jenna's rubbing off on me." Garrett grinned. "She's the most common sense, grounded person I've ever known. It's like God created her just to keep me anchored."

"I want what you two have." Brant winced. "I thought I could have it with Tori."

"That could still work out." Garrett adjusted his cowboy hat as they rounded the pasture and headed back toward the house. "In the meantime, you don't need to base your Nashville or Dallas decision on Tori. We've talked about what you want. But what about what God wants? With or without Tori, is Country music and touring or Dallas what God wants for you?"

What God wanted for him?

"And to complicate things further, you have a third choice."

"What's that?"

"I gave my record company one of your demos. They want you to tour with me. Be my opening act."

"That's awesome!" All his dreams culminating except the one he really wanted—Tori.

"This is probably a stupid question, but have you prayed about making a decision?"

The question sucker-punched Brant in the gut. He'd prayed for a chance at a relationship with Tori. And prayed for a rodeo break to get him into a megachurch. But not once had he asked what God wanted him to do.

The patio door opened in the distance and Jenna stepped out.

"Let me see if she needs something." Garrett urged the horse to a trot.

Brant fell in beside him and the horses ate up the distance. Soon they stopped at the fence.

"Sorry to interrupt, but Mitch just called." Jenna cupped her hands around her mouth. "They disciplined the officer who was supposed to let Mitch know if Russ was released, and they picked Desiree up for aiding and abetting."

"What about her baby?" Garrett dismounted.

"That's what I asked. Social services took him, but Mitch called Quinn and Lacie Remington. They've been fostering teens the last few years, so they agreed to step in and foster the baby."

"Good. I've wondered about that poor child. Desiree is not mother material."

"I'll get out of your hair." Brant dismounted.

"We're not done, are we?" Garrett stroked his horse's muzzle.

"Actually, we are. Thanks for the advice." He tipped his hat in Jenna's direction. "Keep me updated on Tori?"

"Of course." Jenna nodded. "But she's looking for her own place, so she may not be in the guesthouse much longer."

A step toward moving on with her life.

Please Lord, let her change her mind. He didn't even want to think about staying away from her for a lifetime.

No. He needed to turn his relationship with Tori over

to God. If they were meant to be, God would make it happen. He needed focus. And prayer time—to figure out what God wanted him to do.

It was really hard for Brant to lead the congregation in a song he knew by heart with the piano player doing her best to ignore him. It had been this way since his proposal, especially after she officially turned him down. For the past two months, they'd both shown up at every service and done their jobs. But it was passionless.

And on top of that, he had the announcement to make this morning.

Tori had worn a pinched expression throughout the service and it didn't get any better as the altar call wound to a close.

All the prayer warriors returned to their seats and the pastor closed the service in prayer.

"Our song leader needs to make an announcement before we dismiss." Brother Thomas halted the congregation as they began spilling out of the sanctuary.

Brant strode to the podium. "When I came here—I'll admit I didn't plan on staying long. I only came to Aubrey to fulfill my contract at the Stockyard Championship Rodeo. I hoped I'd get a break there and end up at a megachurch.

"But a funny thing happened." He scanned the congregation—his family—and now he had to leave them behind. "I got attached and now that I really don't want to go anywhere, I have three offers. A country music contract in Nashville, a chance to be worship leader at megachurch in Dallas and a chance to go on the road with Garrett as his opening act."

Hushed silence and then scattered applause started up. Soon the entire congregation clapped for him—fully supporting him in whatever direction he went.

"Y'all aren't making this easy. In the last several months, I've come to love each of you and I've rediscovered my love for hymnbooks and traditional churches." Brant stepped down from the stage. "Nashville was easy to turn down since I never wanted to sing Country music anyway. With much prayer, God made me realize I don't want to read words on the wall and lead a praise band. So with His approval, I accepted the offer to tour with Garrett."

The congregation applauded again.

"I'm excited and sad." Brant wanted to look back at Tori—to gauge her reaction, but he kept his focus on the pews. "During my three-month tour with Garrett, my church attendance here will be sketchy. And since you need a full-time song leader, I'm stepping down at the end of this month. I'll miss spending every Sunday here, but Aubrey has become my home and when I'm home, you'll find me here every time the doors are open."

A moan came from behind him and Brant turned to see Tori doubled over on the piano bench.

"I'm sorry." Her words came through clenched teeth. "But I think I'm in labor."

Chapter 16

"What's taking so long?" Brant paced the waiting room. "Isn't she early? It's only the middle of October. And her body's been through so much trauma."

"Only four weeks early." Raquel patted his arm. "And the doctor said the baby's fully developed. Tori's so tiny, the baby probably just ran out of room and decided to make an early appearance. If you don't sit down, people will think you're the father," Raquel whispered.

He didn't really care what anyone thought, but he settled next to his sister.

"Jenna and her aunt are with her. Don't worry. These things take time."

Since Garrett Steele was one of the visitors, the waiting room had been secured and turned into a private area with clusters of anxious church members dotting the room. Natalie and Lane were there, even though they knew Tori had decided to keep her baby. Garrett had told Brant this morning that the couple had applied to adopt Desiree's son and then found out Natalie was pregnant. God had great timing with good news.

"You really love her." Raquel squeezed his arm.

"Yes."

"Have you told her that?"

"Yes."

"And?"

"She turned me down when I proposed to her."

"You proposed?"

"Yep."

"But I ran into her a few months ago. I told her how much you loved her and that at first I thought you were just remembering Tiffany."

Brant's chest squeezed. "You told her about Tiffany?"

"I assumed you had." Raquel clamped a hand over her mouth. "Oh no. I don't know why I can't keep my mouth shut. You know with patient confidentiality, I have no problem. But with life, I'm constantly running off at the mouth—talking faster than I think."

"It doesn't matter."

"But it does." Raquel covered her face with her hands. "Don't you see—she probably thinks you proposed because you felt sorry for her—like you did Tiffany. Or even worse—that she's just a substitute for Tiffany."

"Why would she think either of those things?"

"It's how the female brain works." Raquel rolled her eyes. "I can't believe you finally fall in love and I go and blow it with my big mouth. I can talk to her if you want."

"Uh—no thanks."

Raquel winced. "Guess I've said enough, huh?"

"Don't worry." He put an arm around her shoulders. "I've been praying about Tori. If we're meant to be, it'll work out. Right now, I just need to know everything's all right in there."

The waiting room door opened and Jenna stepped out wearing a huge smile. "Mother and daughter are both fine."

Sighs of relief and prayers of thanks went up. Brant's was the loudest.

"Can we see them?" Raquel asked.

"Tori's getting freshened up, but the baby's in the nursery if anyone wants to come see her."

People trailed out of the waiting room—even Garrett.

But staff had been warned about the famous visitor and a couple of security guards waited in the hall of the hospital.

Aunt Loretta met them at the long panel of windows. A nurse held a baby swaddled in pink with the card in the nearby bassinet—Baby Eaton.

A tiny little sweetheart with perfect features and a tuft of downy copper hair. The only thing she was missing was a name. Along with his last name.

Tori's friends trickled back to the waiting room—probably went home. Even Garrett. But Brant stayed until only he, Jenna and Loretta remained.

"She's a beauty, just like her mama was." Aunt Loretta sniffed and dabbed at her eyes.

"I'd like to see Tori," Brant whispered.

"We'll check and see if she's up to a visit." Jenna and Aunt Loretta headed for her room and Brant longed to do the same. Instead, he focused on the tiny baby.

Finally, after what seemed like hours, the ladies returned.

Aunt Loretta shot him a wink. "She's tuckered out and may be asleep by the time you get there, but she said you can come in."

That had to be a good sign. Brant's hopes latched on to the highest star in the night sky.

Weights sat on Tori's eyelids. But she had to check on her baby. By sheer will, she opened her eyes.

Brant sat in the chair beside her bed. Oh yeah, she'd drifted off after Aunt Loretta asked if he could come in. "Is she okay?"

"She's fine. Aunt Loretta and Jenna went to the nursery to fuss over her."

"I want her with me."

"You need to rest. And you were doing a fine job of it—snoring and drooling."

She grinned and her eyes drifted closed. But she couldn't sleep. Not now.

Brant was here. He'd stayed until her baby was born. If only his past couldn't trouble them. If only her past couldn't plague them as well. If they both had clean slates, she'd jump at the chance of a future with him.

"Raquel told me you know about Tiffany."

"It doesn't matter." Her heart couldn't take this topic. She closed her eyes again.

"It does matter. Tiffany was the pastor's daughter at the church where I grew up. And she was my first crush, but she was dating my best friend. They broke up and she came to me for help. She was pregnant and she wanted me to help her get an abortion."

Tori opened her eyes. A glutton for punishment—she needed to see the emotions playing over his face.

"I told her how I felt about her, that I'd marry her, and raise her baby as mine. We were supposed to tell her folks the next day, but she wound up in the hospital instead. I guess she got scared and didn't want to disappoint her folks, so she had the abortion. But something went wrong." He frowned.

"She died three days later. I blamed myself for a long time, but over the last few years, I've finally come to terms with it. I did everything I could to help her, none of it was my fault—the abortion or her death."

"I'm sorry."

"Me, too." Brant focused on Tori again. "But none of it has anything to do with you. I'm not trying to repeat history. I'm not trying to make up for what happened with Tiffany. My feelings for you have nothing to do with Tiffany."

Could she trust Brant's feelings for her? She closed her eyes again.

"I love you, Tori." He took her hand in his. "And I love

that baby girl down the hall because she's part of you. But I wanted to marry you even when you were planning to give her up. Because I love you—with or without your daughter."

Resist. She had to resist him. "Did Lane and Natalie seem okay?"

"They were great."

"I'm so glad she's pregnant and they're planning to adopt Desiree's baby. They'll be great parents."

"You'll be a great mom, too."

The door opened and a nurse entered holding the baby. Aunt Loretta and Jenna followed. "Can I hold her?" Brant asked.

The nurse looked past him and he turned back to Tori. She nodded.

"Now, be sure and support her head." Aunt Loretta passed the tiny bundle to him.

"How long's it been since you ate, Aunt Loretta? I'm worried about your blood sugar." Tori could barely take her eyes off Brant and her daughter.

"Are you diabetic?" Concern coated Jenna's words.

"Hypoglycemic. But I'm fine."

"Jenna, will you take her to the cafeteria and make sure she eats?"

"I'm on it." Jenna opened the door.

Aunt Loretta blew out a heavy sigh, but followed.

"Take your time." Brant slipped his finger into the baby's hand. "What's your name, beautiful?"

"Lorraine Jana Eaton. After the two women who've supported me through everything, but unique for her."

"A beautiful name for a beautiful princess." Brant hummed a tune and two-stepped around the room in grand swoops. Totally enchanted with her daughter. "She's gonna be a fiesty redhead just like her momma."

God had tried to give her the gift of this man. A man

who loved her. And obviously loved Lorraine. It was time to forget the past and take the gift.

"Brant?"

"Hmm?"

"Is that offer you made still out there?"

"What offer is that?" His attention never left Lorraine's face as he continued his dance.

"Your proposal?"

His dance came to an abrupt halt and his gaze caught hers. "Most definitely."

"I'd like to marry you."

"You would?" A slow grin pulled at his mouth. He approached her bed and bent closer to capture her lips. With Lorraine nestled between them, he teased Tori with a tender kiss. She curled her arms around his neck and pulled him closer. The caress of his lips deepened and he kissed her right out of her socks.

A wail rose up between them.

Brant jerked away and jostled Lorraine. "Sorry, little lady, I didn't mean to mash you, but your momma just made my day."

"I think she's hungry."

"Oh, where's her bottle? I can feed her."

"Um." Tori's face heated. "I don't think you're equipped for that."

Brant's face turned purple. "Oh. Um, yeah, I'll get out of here." He handed Lorraine over and backed toward the door. "But, you're not gonna change your mind again, are you?"

"After that kiss—not on your life."

"Hmm. I didn't know it was that powerful. I'll have to remember that." He grinned and with an exaggerated swagger, he left the room.

The church was decorated with pink roses, yards of tulle, ribbon and lace. Family and friends smiled their approval and support as Tori entered the sanctuary. Holding six-week-old Lorraine, Brant waited at the front of the church.

Her satin dress and his dove-gray tux were straight from the dream she'd had a few months back. Just like her dream. Except he faced her. And nothing could ruin this dream. It wasn't a dream. It was her reality.

And the perfect day for their wedding—Thanksgiving. So much to be thankful for.

Yesterday, the judge had finalized adoption proceedings making Brant Lorraine's father. In every sense of the word. The perfect wedding gift. The perfect wedding. Followed by a honeymoon in Cancún—a present from Garrett and Jenna—along with a nanny for the trip since Tori couldn't even imagine leaving Lorraine at home.

Her business was up and running and she'd found a great manager. In a month, they'd leave for Brant's three-month tour with Garrett. The future blinded her with promise.

She stopped at Brant's side and slipped her fingers into the crook of his arm. His bicep resonated with both strength and gentleness. Brant kissed her cheek and then ever so gently brushed his lips across Lorraine's forehead.

Tori buried her nose in her daughter's downy hair. All of this had happened while Brant was looking for his rodeo break. Instead, God had given Tori and Lorraine a break—the blessing of Brant's love. And their rodeo family.

* * * * *

REQUEST YOUR FREE BOOKS!

2 FREE INSPIRATIONAL NOVELS
PLUS 2
FREE
MYSTERY GIFTS

Love Inspired

YES! Please send me 2 FREE Love Inspired® novels and my 2 FREE mystery gifts (gifts are worth about $10). After receiving them, if I don't wish to receive any more books, I can return the shipping statement marked "cancel." If I don't cancel, I will receive 6 brand-new novels every month and be billed just $4.74 per book in the U.S. or $5.24 per book in Canada. That's a savings of at least 21% off the cover price. It's quite a bargain! Shipping and handling is just 50¢ per book in the U.S. and 75¢ per book in Canada.* I understand that accepting the 2 free books and gifts places me under no obligation to buy anything. I can always return a shipment and cancel at any time. Even if I never buy another book, the two free books and gifts are mine to keep forever.

105/305 IDN F49N

Name _____ (PLEASE PRINT)

Address _____ Apt. #

City _____ State/Prov. _____ Zip/Postal Code

Signature (if under 18, a parent or guardian must sign)

Mail to the Harlequin® Reader Service:
IN U.S.A.: P.O. Box 1867, Buffalo, NY 14240-1867
IN CANADA: P.O. Box 609, Fort Erie, Ontario L2A 5X3

Are you a subscriber to Love Inspired books
and want to receive the larger-print edition?
Call 1-800-873-8635 or visit www.ReaderService.com.

* Terms and prices subject to change without notice. Prices do not include applicable taxes. Sales tax applicable in N.Y. Canadian residents will be charged applicable taxes. Offer not valid in Quebec. This offer is limited to one order per household. Not valid for current subscribers to Love Inspired books. All orders subject to credit approval. Credit or debit balances in a customer's account(s) may be offset by any other outstanding balance owed by or to the customer. Please allow 4 to 6 weeks for delivery. Offer available while quantities last.

Your Privacy—The Harlequin® Reader Service is committed to protecting your privacy. Our Privacy Policy is available online at www.ReaderService.com or upon request from the Harlequin Reader Service.
We make a portion of our mailing list available to reputable third parties that offer products we believe may interest you. If you prefer that we not exchange your name with third parties, or if you wish to clarify or modify your communication preferences, please visit us at www.ReaderService.com/consumerchoice or write to us at Harlequin Reader Service Preference Service, P.O. Box 9062, Buffalo, NY 14269. Include your complete name and address.

LIDIR13R

REQUEST YOUR FREE BOOKS!

2 FREE INSPIRATIONAL NOVELS
PLUS 2
FREE
MYSTERY GIFTS

Love Inspired.
HISTORICAL
INSPIRATIONAL HISTORICAL ROMANCE

YES! Please send me 2 FREE Love Inspired® Historical novels and my 2 FREE mystery gifts (gifts are worth about $10). After receiving them, if I don't wish to receive any more books, I can return the shipping statement marked "cancel." If I don't cancel, I will receive 4 brand-new novels every month and be billed just $4.74 per book in the U.S. or $5.24 per book in Canada. That's a savings of at least 21% off the cover price. It's quite a bargain! Shipping and handling is just 50¢ per book in the U.S. and 75¢ per book in Canada.* I understand that accepting the 2 free books and gifts places me under no obligation to buy anything. I can always return a shipment and cancel at any time. Even if I never buy another book, the two free books and gifts are mine to keep forever.

102/302 IDN F5CY

Name	(PLEASE PRINT)	
Address		Apt. #
City	State/Prov.	Zip/Postal Code

Signature (if under 18, a parent or guardian must sign)

Mail to the Harlequin® Reader Service:
IN U.S.A.: P.O. Box 1867, Buffalo, NY 14240-1867
IN CANADA: P.O. Box 609, Fort Erie, Ontario L2A 5X3

Want to try two free books from another series?
Call 1-800-873-8635 or visit www.ReaderService.com.

* Terms and prices subject to change without notice. Prices do not include applicable taxes. Sales tax applicable in N.Y. Canadian residents will be charged applicable taxes. Offer not valid in Quebec. This offer is limited to one order per household. Not valid for current subscribers to Love Inspired Historical books. All orders subject to credit approval. Credit or debit balances in a customer's account(s) may be offset by any other outstanding balance owed by or to the customer. Please allow 4 to 6 weeks for delivery. Offer available while quantities last.

Your Privacy—The Harlequin® Reader Service is committed to protecting your privacy. Our Privacy Policy is available online at www.ReaderService.com or upon request from the Harlequin Reader Service.

We make a portion of our mailing list available to reputable third parties that offer products we believe may interest you. If you prefer that we not exchange your name with third parties, or if you wish to clarify or modify your communication preferences, please visit us at www.ReaderService.com/consumerchoice or write to us at Harlequin Reader Service Preference Service, P.O. Box 9062, Buffalo, NY 14269. Include your complete name and address.

LIHDIR13R